I0601136

UNDER AN OUTBACK SKY

EDGE OF THE OUTBACK ROMANCE

SUZANNE GILCHRIST

MALLEE STAR ENTERPRISES

This is a work of fiction. Names, characters and incidents depicted in this book are the products of the author's imagination or are used fictitiously. Any resemblance to actual events, locales, organisations, or persons, living or

Cover Design by: Patti Roberts of Paradox Book Design

First published in 2013 by: Mallee Star Enterprises Queensland, Australia

Written in Australian English

ACKNOWLEDGEMENT OF COUNTRY

In the spirit of reconciliation, the author and publisher acknowledges Aboriginal and Torres Strait Islander peoples as the First Australians and Traditional Custodians of the lands where we live, learn and work. We pay our respects to Elders past and present and all First Nations peoples and honour their unique cultural and spiritual relationships to the lands, waters and seas and their rich contribution to society, and for their ongoing custodianship of and care for Country.

OTHER BOOKS BY THE AUTHOR

Bargain with the Enemy

Touring the Stars

The Slave Trap

Mars Academy Series:

Stranded

Cosmic Fire

Apocalyptic/Dystopian:

Paying the Forfeit

Storm of Fire

Don't Look Back (Warders of Earth)

Quest for Earth

CONTEMPORARY

Bindarra Creek Makeover (Bindarra Creek Romance)

Desire for Love

Scent of the Jaguar (Deadly Forces series)

Cotton Field Dreams (Mindalby Outback Romance)

FANTASY/ANCIENT WORLDS EROTIC ROMANCE

Bound by Love

Bound by Lies

DEDICATION

For mum. For my children.
Now and always.

Edge of the Outback Romance Series
Cowboy Under the Mistletoe
Dance in the Outback
The Cowboy's Gift
Under an Outback Sky

ONE

"Paper cowboy heading your way, over."

The two-way radio crackled to life rousing Maggie Hayes from her heat-induced doze. She swung her bare feet down from where they rested on the countertop and straightened in the chair. Fighting a yawn, she reached for the mic of the ham radio reposing on the shelf beside her, mumbling, "Say again, over."

"Look sharp, Maggie. He's already outside the store. Remember. Suss him out. We've got to know what he's up to."

"I'm all over it, Snake. Over and out." Maggie flung the mic onto the counter, brushed back her long curly hair, and rose to her feet.

A man pushed through the fly strips hanging motionless in the doorway. Pausing, he made use of the hand sanitiser placed strategically on a stool just inside the shop. Seconds later, his boots rang out as he crossed the lino-covered floor with purposeful strides, heading directly for her.

She soaked up the unexpected images of wide shoulders and a firm chest covered by an immaculate buttoned-up white linen shirt tucked neatly into buckskin Linesman jeans that outlined muscular thighs. Her gaze ran over his lean body again and she sucked in a breath, her heart beating extremely fast.

He moved towards the counter with the ease and grace of a man in his prime. He had to be no older than late thirties perhaps. She checked out his boots, noting the hard-looking brand new leather. Actually, everything he wore looked brand new.

Definitely a paper cowboy.

Was Snake right? There had been a rumour flying around town the past couple of weeks that a gas mining company rep was checking out the local area. Although Maggie had yet to confirm that rumour with her own eyes. Maybe this bloke was the rep? Whoever he was, Maggie knew she'd never seen him before in her life. There was no way she'd ever forget those midnight dark eyes of his and the way they seemed to twinkle like he had a true zest for life.

Twinkle? Am I crazy?

She pinned her best smile to her lips, calling out a cheery, "Good morning. Anything I can help you with?"

He plucked a buff-coloured Akubra off his head that looked like he'd just taken it off the shelf and fanned his slightly flushed face. A grimace turned down the corners of his well-shaped mouth. "Some relief from this heat would be good. Don't you have air-conditioning?" His frowning gaze travelled around the store, no doubt taking in the aisles empty of shoppers, the small display of sweating fruit and vegetables, and the thick, insulated door at the rear that led to the walk-in freezer where the meat and dairy products were stocked, then back to her.

Someone has had a bad day. With difficulty, she kept her expression open and friendly. "It's on the blink. We're waiting for a tech to come over from Walgett."

He grimaced before giving a tight smile. "Sorry, excuse my whingeing. I'm just back from a stint in Antarctica and finding it hard to adjust to early Australian summer."

"Really? How fascinating. What, are you like - an explorer? A scientist?" Leaning forward, Maggie eyed him with fresh interest.

He took a hasty step backwards. "Nothing so glamorous. Merely one of a team that keeps the station running. I'm after some cold water," he added, abruptly cutting short any idea Maggie may have had of continuing that line of conversation.

Bit of a mystery man then.

Her mind whirled. Were there gas deposits in Antarctica? Surely mining wasn't allowed in the vast southern continent. She made a mental note to do some serious researching on the net as soon as she was alone.

She jerked a thumb sideways. "Over on your right there's a drink refrigerator behind the last aisle."

"Cheers." He strode off. A few seconds later, he retraced his footsteps back to the counter, water bottle in hand. "How much do I owe you?"

After Maggie had handed back his change, she tried again. Snake could be wrong. The stranger could have nothing whatsoever to do with the mining company.

Simply someone passing through. But passing through from where? Sturt's Crossing was a long, long way from Antarctica. A long way from anywhere really. Which made it all the more curious as to who he was and what he was doing in their tiny country town.

"So, what brings you to Sturt's Crossing?"

"No particular reason." He shrugged and turning appeared to take a second and longer look at the empty shop. "Doesn't appear to be many people about. How many still live here in town?"

Maggie frowned as she closed the cash register. "Enough." He wasn't the only one who could clam up.

His eyes arrowed onto her and stayed.

Heat spread over her face and she shuffled her feet imagining how she must look. Red hair, freckles...and now red cheeks. Perfect if you were a tomato.

She delicately cleared her throat. "Staying at the pub?"

He sighed and pressed the cold bottle against his forehead. "Yeah. My room is upstairs, above the front bar. I thought it'd be quiet, but the owner has a fondness for ABBA songs played what seems like all night long."

Maggie laughed. "That's Snake's dad, Charlie. He's semi-retired but still likes to hang out with the locals."

"No closing time then?"

"Sure. Ten pm sharp. But in summer Charlie kips down in the cellar where its cooler. I guess he likes having music played while he sleeps. You could ask him to turn it down."

"I did - then last night it was louder than before," he said wryly.

Thinking fast, she tilted her head and pursed her lips. "If you're staying in town for a few days I know a comfy B&B that might suit you better. It's got solar power and you can run the air conditioner in the bedroom day and night." Pulse kicking up a beat, she crossed her fingers and went for the final kicker. "Unfortunately, the motel is closed for another two months. Nicole and Kevin – they're the owners – are doing some serious re-modelling."

"I'd never have thought there'd be sufficient tourists to warrant doing even the smallest amount of renos." His voice echoed his disbelief.

Maggie kept her neutral smile in place. "Oh, we have plans to open up this entire region to tourists. Covid lockdowns of course put a bit of a dint in our agenda, but we'll get there. It won't be long, and this will be the latest holiday hot spot."

"If you say so." He replaced his hat over his tousled black hair, the brim shadowing the expression in his eyes. "I like the idea of a B&B. What's the food like?"

"Excellent, considering I'm the cook." Smiling, she all but skipped out from behind the counter. A few discreet tugs and she'd soothed the creases in the loose white cotton shirt she wore over faded blue jeans. "I'll show you the room now, if you like."

He nodded and fell into step as she hurried to the door hoping he wouldn't change his mind.

Having him in the house where she also lived, could lead to more opportunities to grill him about his inten-tions. Plus, the extra money would come in handy for her friend, Rosie – not to mention Maggie herself would receive a small percentage of the funds as remuneration for her role as manager. Win, win all round.

Grabbing her straw hat from a hook beside the open door, she slid through the vinyl fly strips and waited on the footpath for the bloke to join her.

"Not going to lock up?" Disbelief rang clear in his tone.

"All good." She clapped her wide-brimmed, floppy hat onto her head. "This way. What's your name?"

Was it her imagination or did he hesitate a beat before answering?

"John. John Jones."

"Uh huh." She shot him a sideways glance as they walked down the empty road. "I'm Maggie Hayes."

"Lived here all your life?"

"Yes." She raised her face to the burning sun and smiled before lowering her head from its hot kiss. "My family own the store and I run it now. They've currently in Port Stephens."

They strode along the gravel road in silence.

"Ever done any travelling? Or lived somewhere else? Sorry, but I can't help but think I've seen you or met you somewhere before."

Panic squeezed her throat for a split second. It was probably silly of her to feel embarrassed, but she couldn't help it. Swallowing, she managed an airy, "I must have one of those faces."

"Right."

His tone told her louder than words he didn't totally believe her. But what the heck? She didn't believe him either. *John Jones*. Now, that was a made-up name if she'd ever heard one!

She snuck another sideways peek at his profile, biting back a sigh. She'd read about *'chiselled jaws'* and here was the living proof such a thing existed.

What a pity if he turned out to be the enemy.

CHAPTER

TWO

R osie's house was mid-way down Coolibah Street which ran parallel to Sturt's Crossing's main road. It meant a trudge along a wide, gravel road with little relief from the heat of a blazing midday sun that seared from the hard-packed ground as if the road was a hotplate. As they came closer, Maggie couldn't repress the smile that sprung to her lips as her gaze absorbed the property. Built in the 1920's, the house was an old Californian-style bungalow made from red brick that had been transported into the town from the east coast. The front porch was wide and spread across the entire front of the house. The perfect place to enjoy a refreshing cool drink and watch the stars appear in the inky darkness of the night sky.

After Rosie had acquired it as part of her deceased godmother's estate, her friend had made a few improvements. A new colour-bond roof in a shade called '*Paperbark*' had replaced the old rusting iron sheets. The off-white gutters were also new as were the freshly painted white window trimmings. The old broken-down fence was gone and in its place was a hedge of wild rosemary bushes. A mulga tree had been planted in the front yard and beneath it sat a stone bird bath that Maggie religiously filled with treated bore water every day. It was wonderful to start the day with the twittering of bird song and fun to watch the lorikeets and budgies toss water around as they enjoyed a cooling bath. The grass was sparse but recently mown with the rich red earth of the Outback forming a vivid contrast to its dusty olive-green growth. On either side of the steps, reposed a large ceramic pot filled with flowering blood-red Sturt desert peas.

"Here we are," she said as she stepped onto the freshly swept concrete path that led to the house. From inside the house, came a muffled 'woof'.

"Doesn't look too bad." Mystery man fell in behind her.

"Yes. Rosie and her husband, Luke, have done a fabulous job in restoring some of the original features. Of course, there's still a bit of work to be done."

"Mmmm. You did say there was air-conditioning? And what about sufficient water for a shower every day?"

"Don't worry, Mr Jones. I'm a woman of my word." Pausing on the top step of the veranda, she turned to meet his eyes. "Showering every day is fine, but I'd appreciate if you use the timer in the bathroom. It's set for three minutes max. We're on strict water restrictions."

He nodded. "Understood. I'm used to living with limited resources."

"I'll hold you to that." She raised her chin in silent challenge. "Since I live on the premises, I'll be monitoring your usage."

"I had no idea this was your house."

"It isn't. I manage it for my friend Rosie and in return, I get rent-free accommodation." Plus, it was so much more comfortable than living in the shipping container housing she'd grown up in and that abutted the back of the store.

"Sounds like a good arrangement." He gestured toward the house. "Shall we go inside? I'd like to take a quick look before I commit to staying here."

Flushing, she crossed to the unlocked front door and opened it. "Of course."

Inside, the house was a typical Californian design with a hallway running down the centre and rooms opening off both sides. She waved a hand to the left. "Through here is the main living room which as you can see, opens past that archway to the formal dining area. I hope you like dogs. That's Sherman lounging in front of the air con."

A scruffy wire-haired terrier lifted his head, opened one eye and thumped his tail, before slumping back into his comfy-looking dog bed strategically placed below the wall air conditioning unit.

"He won't give you any trouble. Now, the four guest bedrooms are all on the right-hand side as is the main bathroom which is the third door along the hall and in-between the bedrooms. It's shared but there is an additional cloakroom running off the laundry which is at the back of the house. I hope sharing the facilities won't be a problem?"

Flicking a quick glance over her shoulder, Maggie saw him shake his head as he went into the living room to take a good look around. After allowing him another few seconds, she continued to walk along the hall.

"You can have your pick of the bedrooms. I do have a booking for next Monday for one of the rooms but as I'm uncertain of how long you'll be in town...?" She allowed her voice to trail suggestively off but he didn't rise to the bait.

Emerging out into the hall, he grunted noncommittally.

Folding her arms over her waist, she waited while he inspected each room with painstaking thoroughness.

"I'll take this one on the other side of the bathroom if that's alright with you."

She smiled, some of her tension dissipating. Thank heavens. A paying guest. But for how long?

"I'll need some details from you first then I'll give you a key and let you retrieve your bags from the pub. Behind the house, there's a big carport which fronts the next street, where you can park your car out of the sun. On the bedside table in your room, you'll find a folder that has information on the town and the surrounding area as well as details about the wi-fi login. Feel free to use the television or radio although we only pick up the ABC out here." She grinned. "But there's plenty of DVD's and lots of books in the library – that's the room opposite the kitchen."

"You said you live here too. Where's your room? I don't want to unintentionally intrude on your privacy."

"Um..." She turned hastily away to hide the vivid blush on her face. "I've got a bedroom and a small office at the end of the house. You won't hear any ABBA songs from me in the middle of the night."

"Good to know. There's only so much of the 'Dancing Queen' a bloke can take."

Maggie laughed. "Let's get the paperwork done then. This way." Turning to lead the way to the office, she couldn't repress a satisfied smirk. Now, she'd find out his true identity.

However she was foiled as her visitor scrawled some completely illegible signature on the paper and popped in 'John Jones' as his name. Frowning over the page, Maggie muttered, "Is that it? What about an address? I'll need one in case I have to chase you for unpaid bills."

"Won't be a problem. I'll pay with cash for a week in advance." John then proceeded to count out the bills before laying them on the desk. "Satisfied?"

"Not really," she grumbled as she thumbed through the fifty-dollar notes. Who carried cash these days? Narrowing her eyes, she glared at him and handed over the receipt she took off the printer. "This will cover the room and breakfast. Dinner is extra."

"I'd like to pay for any meals on a daily basis. I may take dinner over at the pub a few times."

Shrugging, she turned aside to place the money in a cash tin. "Suit yourself. Just let me know each morning of your intentions. I'll pop fresh towels in your room then leave you to it. If you need anything, my mobile number is on the receipt. I'll be in the store for the rest of the day. Are you eating here tonight?"

"No. I think since I'm checking out of the pub, I'll eat there today."

"Fair enough. Snake can use the custom and Egon, he's the pub's cook, does amazing barbeque beef spareribs on Thursday nights. At least, that's what I've been told. I don't eat out that often. I have to warn you, though, about tomorrow night which as it's Friday the pub may get a bit rowdy. Some of the road crew will probably come into town to let off steam."

"Road crew?"

"Yes. There's a gang camping out along the road toward Tibooburra where they're working on tarring the last section. It'll be great for the locals and for tourists once it's finished."

"Are they planning on tarring all the way into Sturt National Park?"

Maggie shook her head. "I'm not certain but I think not at this stage."

"Pity. It's a beautiful park."

"Have you visited it already?"

"Not this time around. I did some camping in the park many years ago." He gave a curt nod as he stuffed his wallet into his pocket. "If that's everything, I'll get my gear and move in."

"I'll see you later then. Have a great day," she called out to his disappearing back as he left the office.

After locking the cash tin in the floor safe, and shutting down her laptop, Maggie wandered into the kitchen where she re-filled Sherman's water bowl. Taking a cold, unlabelled, brown glass bottle out of the refrigerator she stood for a moment thinking about her new guest. With a rueful shake of the head, she told herself she had work to do.

But as she returned to the store with her drink in hand, she couldn't help thinking that she had more questions than answers about a certain *'John Jones'*.

CHAPTER

THREE

F orty minutes later, Jace aka John Jones had settled his tab at the pub (much to Snake's disappointment) and moved his car and gear over to the B&B. As he wheeled his luggage bag inside the bedroom he'd chosen, he gave a satisfied sigh. Peace and quiet. Miles away from anyone who knew him. Exactly what he wanted. Sturt's Crossing was too damn far for anyone to think about dragging their sorry butts through the Outback to hunt him down and spew guilt onto his head. No one cared enough to do such a thing anyway. He'd made certain of that – pushing what little remained of his family away until they rarely bothered to make contact. Unless it was when the date of Douglas's anniversary rolled around which would be in three day's time. Seventeen years and yet the rawness of his loss was an ache in Jace's heart that wouldn't heal.

The silence in the old house settled on his shoulders and immediately desolation swamped him. Who was he kidding? There'd been a time when all he wanted was to spend time with his family and especially with his only sibling.

Growing up, they'd been inseparable. Douglas, two years older and always a giant in Jace's eyes, never minded his younger brother tagging along, even including him in his footy team at school. He'd always been there for him. They'd ridden their bikes together, played video games and sport together, laughed together, even cried together when their old pet cat had passed away.

He'd been the buffer between Jace and his cold, remote mother who had only rarely displayed a gesture of affection where he was concerned. Although Doug had been the obvious favourite with his mother, Doug never seemed to take it as his due – instead he remained kind and firmly fixed by Jace's side.

Their father had been quite different from their other parent, treating each boy equally and had spent time when he could with both. A man consumed with his career, he had still found time to coach them with soccer and later had taught them both to surf.

And then suddenly those idyllic days of childhood and those awkward years of being pimply teenagers together were destroyed - the memories overshadowed by the dark days that followed. Those feelings of being part of something special – of family - were long gone. Jace had been alone ever since.

Rubbing a hand over his chin, he closed the door and flung himself onto a plush teal-coloured, wing-back armchair. Weariness sank into his bones. It had been a long drive yesterday. The pub's narrow bed with its sagging mattress had ensured his sleep of the night before had been fragmented and uncomfortable. He stretched out his legs in front of him, toeing off his boots. It was a relief to ease out the stiffness in his joints.

The air conditioner hummed quietly on the opposite wall and a heavy stupor weighed him down. Maybe it had been dumb of him to think a place as different from Melbourne as Mars was to Venus could soften the impact of the harrowing memories. But he'd been desperate to escape anywhere that reminded him of what he'd lost and never been able to find again. Not that he'd really tried. And why he'd decided not to give his real name was a conundrum. It was as if by pretending he was someone else, someone entirely different, new even, the past would stop rising up and haunting him.

What a joke. He'd never be free and if he wanted to be honest with himself, he didn't want to be – because if those painful memories faded there would be nothing left. His parents were divorced, had moved on to new partners and families. His mother hardly ever contacted him – his father... Well, that was another festering wound of misery. All the while, time had whittled his memories of Doug away to little more than a handful of images that faded more each day.

He wondered what his new landlord would say if she knew he'd shut his eyes and poked his finger at the map. That was how he'd re-discovered this remote area of western New South Wales and with that one action, a handful of blurred recollections of an almost forgotten camping trip Doug and he had taken with their father many years ago. She'd probably be appalled. Or perhaps amused. She appeared to be an easy-going kind of woman if a little nosy. Plus, she had a very sweet smile and laughing green eyes.

Woah! Steady on there, son.

Laughing eyes?

What was he thinking?

Sinking into the comfortable cushions fatigue hit him like he'd just returned from trekking over the ice for two days. Maybe it was time for catch up on the sleep he'd missed the night before.

Something scratched at the door. Then whined.

The dog.

Sighing, he hauled himself up then moved to the door. Upon opening it, he discovered the scruffy looking dog that had been curled up in the living room the last time he'd seen him. What had the redhead called him? Oh yeah. Sherman.

The dog panted happily, thumping his tail on the floor.

"Fine. Come on in, then." He held the door open a bit wider and the dog scampered inside then began to sniff around his luggage. "Hey! Don't you even think about it. You want to pee, do it outside."

After giving him what he could only call an aggrieved look, Sherman flattened himself on the ground until he looked like an animal skin and peered up out of his hairy eyebrows.

"Good boy." Jace gave the dog a rough fondle around his head, then spent a few moments scratching behind his ears much to Sherman's intense pleasure.

The opening stanza of the movie *Jaws* theme song

flooded the room. Jace stiffened, his gaze shooting to where his mobile lay on the bed. The ringing tone stopped. Squeezing his eyes shut, he waited. Sure enough, the phone rang again. He suspected it wouldn't stop ringing until he answered. Guess now was as good a time as any to face the music.

Snatching up the phone, he paced up and down the room. "Yeah. I'm here."

"And where exactly is here, Jace?" came the shrill agitated voice of his mother.

"Somewhere a long way from you." The words spilled from his lips before he could catch them.

Julie sucked in a sharp breath. "Well. That's certainly telling me, isn't it? I take it you won't be at the memorial service on Saturday."

"No."

"I think it's time you stopped acting like a two-year old who's lost his spade and bucket and get the hell home."

"What home? You destroyed it. All I've got left are poisoned memories."

"That's rubbish and you know it. I did one thing. That's not enough to erase the thirty-eight years of your life."

Jace rubbed his nose wearily. "Yeah right. You did more than that and now everything's tainted. Everything I believed about my life, about me is a lie."

"I'm still your mother. Your father is still your father."

"And yet neither one of you wanted anything to do

with me after Doug died." *And apart from one letter, Dad hasn't contacted me since.*

"I don't understand why you would even think such a thing."

"Really? Dad can't bear to even look at me." Jace pulled the curtain aside and stared blindly out the window.

"We were grieving and you made zero allowances for what we were going through - we're still family even though your father and I are divorced. And Douglas – even though he's gone – he's still your older brother."

Dropping the curtain, he returned to his restless pacing. "Hah! You should have told me. You should have told all of us, including Dad, a long, long time ago. Instead, you kept me a dirty little secret that took Doug becoming seriously ill before you owned it."

"It wasn't the best timing," she admitted slowly.

Jace gave a harsh laugh.

"Talk about an understatement." His fingers clenched over the phone, and he had to fight the urge to fling the damn thing against the wall. Then as if all the energy had been sucked out of him, he stopped his restless pacing and slumped into the armchair. "I've got to go."

"Wait...Jace, come back to Melbourne, and we can talk. Have coffee together."

"It's too late." He pressed the *'end call'* button then turned the phone onto silent. What would his brother think of him, if he could see him now – shunning his parents, shunning his life, hiding from his past?

Well, shunning his mother if truth were to be told.

His father was the one who shunned *him* as if everything that had happened had been his fault. And then Jace had turned his back on the pair of them. He had refused to respond to her few phone calls until the contact had all but dried up completely. But then there'd been that one letter Dad had sent him six months ago and which Jace had yet to open. The letter that he still carried with him inside his suitcase. What if his father had finally reached out to him? What if he wanted to forge a new future with him? What if he simply wanted to spill more anger and undeserving recriminations on Jace's innocent head? What if his father was ill? Needed him?

Suddenly, Jace's own behaviour appeared wanting. For a long time he sat in the shadowed room pummelled with bitter and sweet moments from the past and a squirming regret. For the first time in how long he couldn't remember, not all the memories were dark and brimming with anger and grief. Maybe it was time he faced all that hurt, disillusionment and feelings of abandonment he'd done his best to bury and moved forward. Maybe it was time to open that letter.

His gaze travelled to his suitcase and yet he still couldn't bring himself to shift from the chair. Guilt. Anger. Grief and yeah, probably fear. Soon though. Soon he'd rip open that envelope and finally deal with what he believed would be his father's final rejection.

After which that tiny barely acknowledged hope that he'd once again belong would be extinguished forever.

CHAPTER
FOUR

Maggie looked up when she heard footsteps and waved a cheery hand in greeting to the three senior citizens squeezing through the door.

By dint of banging her walker against the other two ladies' ankles and who howled in protest, Mary Porter managed to push into the lead. In a matter of seconds she fronted Maggie at the counter. Once she got going with that walker and with her new joggers on, no one in town could catch her.

"There should be a speed limit on those things," huffed Mrs. Gwozdek as she wobbled along in her friend's wake in her high heels. She wore her *'going out'* outfit, a pair of leopard print spandex pants and a matching tank under a tatty cardigan. A wide-brimmed Mexican hat pinned with fake flowers completed her ensemble.

Mary put the brakes on then edged around to plonk onto the walker's hard seat. The plastic squeaked in protest. "Oh, hush Rebekah. You're simply jealous that you don't have one." She tossed back her thinning white hair that lay in lank folds to her narrow shoulders.

Rebekah Gwozdek managed a snort that was more of a snuffle and clung to the closest shelf for balance. Peering over the thick black spectacles she was never seen without, she pulled the sides of her rainbow-hued cardigan closer over her bulging chest. She'd been a well-built woman in her prime. Now in old age, gravity was finally having its way as every rounded scrap of skin sagged towards the ground. Yet she still loved wearing body-hugging clothes that were so unforgiving to her figure. Whenever she spoke, her plump jowls quivered and shook in a manner that Maggie found hard to tear her eyes from.

Ignoring the drool seeping from the corner of Ms. Porter's mouth and who looked, judging from her lowered eyelids, as if she'd decided to take a nap, Maggie said in a bright voice, "What can I do for you ladies?"

"You can give us an update on that hunk of a gubba you've snagged for starters." The third and youngest of the small group, Deborah White, known as Aunty Deborah throughout the community helped herself to a chocolate bar. After removing the wrapper, she stuffed it into her mouth as she fixed her dark eyes on Maggie's face. She heaved herself up onto the counter and swung dirty feet clad in a pair of rubber thongs. Aunty Deborah must have spent the morning in her studio because she was liberally splattered with paint. There was even a long streak of bright ochre in her frizzy, greying black hair.

"That's a dollar fifty you owe me." Maggie raised her eyebrows. "And I haven't snagged anyone."

"Then what are you waiting for? I got a good eyeful in my telescope this arvo when I spotted him walking down the street. A fella like that won't be alone for long. He'll be snatched up quicker than old Charlie can swallow his pint of beer." Her dark eyes glinted with glee. "Snake tells me this new bloke will be at the pub tonight having dinner. I fancy a need for some ribs coming on. I could check him out for you."

Aunty Deborah grinned, showing chocolate smeared all over her strong white teeth. She popped another bar into the pocket of the paint-stained apron she wore over skinny short shorts and a just as skimpy tank top that revealed long brown arms and legs. Blessed with smooth caramel skin from her mother's side of the family, she could have passed for a woman in her late fifties – not someone who'd never side the sunny side of seventy again. Apart from having lived in Sturt's Crossing all her life, she was now also a bit of a celebrity in artistic circles thanks to a rising global demand for her paintings.

Maggie should know as she and Snake managed her artist website and dealt with her orders. "Constable Anderson said you were to stop using your telescope to spy on people."

"Him! Wouldn't know up from down. Now how about I suss him out. Find out if he's married and or got any kiddies." Grinning, Aunty Deborah primped her short hair with a hand speckled with paint, leaving behind another smear of orange and red.

"Oh, please don't," implored Maggie. She could just

imagine that conversation! With more than a little desperation she focussed on a more important matter. "How's the latest piece going? I'd love to feature it on my vlog when it's ready."

After glowering at a point above Maggie's head for several silent seconds, Aunty Deborah finally muttered, "I don't think I'm happy with it. The boulders are looking more like mud pools than rocks."

"I'm sure it will be wonderful. Like all your paintings."

Looking uncomfortable, the renowned artist hunched her shoulders then with a sly grin poked her finger in Mary Porter's back causing the other old woman to snap her eyes open and yelp. "Wake up, Mary."

"Where was I?" Mary took a slow look around the store before her blurry gaze settled on Maggie. "I know. I remember. Have you heard any more news from your parents?"

"Nah. Yeah. Well, not really from Mum or Dad but Glen sent me a text message this morning telling me they'll be home next week."

"Is that so?" Mary Porter aimed a superior 'told you so' smirk towards her friends. "Thought they said they'd be spending the rest of their active years touring this great land of ours. I told Lucy when she first mentioned this hair-brained idea – mark my words, I give it a month and you'll be sick of the sight of each other. There's nothing worse than having a man under your feet night and day. I told her – she'll be back before she knew it."

Struggling to maintain a pleasant expression, Maggie

took the proffered five-dollar note from Aunty Deborah and opened the till.

Mrs. Gwozdek sucked in a delighted breath. "Sounds like they've had enough of life on the road. Looks like you were right Mary."

Barely managing to stop herself from rolling her eyes, Maggie said through her teeth, "They're flying home for a visit. That's all."

"Flying? That would cost a pretty penny." Ms. Porter shared a knowing look at the other two ladies. "Have they sold that enormous house on wheels?"

"No. Jacko and Glen were working on a horse stud in Scone which isn't too far from Port Stephens. Glen is going to drive my parents' motorhome to Sturt's Crossing while Jacko drives his Landcruiser back."

"A bit odd if you ask me. Are you sure there's nothing wrong? I bet it's gout. Men always get gout when they reach a certain age." Mrs. Gwozdek clucked her tongue in a sympathetic fashion.

"I assure you Dad doesn't have gout," Maggie bit out, wishing they'd all go away and leave her alone.

Mary Porter gave a solemn nod. "Divorce. I warned Lucy living hand and foot with a man is not a good idea."

"*No one* is getting a divorce!"

Aunty Deborah reached over and patted Maggie's hand. "Now, now dear. Don't get in a tizzy. Are they home for good is what I want to know."

Getting frustrated with these lovely but nosy old biddies was a lost cause. Maggie managed a smile. "I have no idea, to be honest. But I know my parents were keen to do the Birdsville Track so maybe they intend to head that way next."

All three old ladies exchanged loaded glances that almost sent Maggie's blood pressure through the roof. Before she could explode however, Aunty Deborah said, "Any chance that rascally brother of yours can take over from you for a while? It would do you good, lovey, to have a break."

"No life for a young girl," Ms. Porter interjected, her rheumy eyes like twin blue beads as she stared hard at Maggie.

Mid-thirties was hardly being a young girl. She had loads of time ahead of her to pursue her dreams.

Hadn't she?

Maggie worked hard not to reveal her own secret misgivings. "I'm quite content minding the store, thank you."

"Don't get on your high horse." Aunty Deborah held up her hands in surrender and slid off the counter. "We've got your best interests in mind, lovey. Someone has to look out for you."

"That's very kind of all of you but not necessary."

"Hmmm. Well time will tell. Anyway, what we've come to tell you is that we're more than happy to help in any way we can. If your parents take off again and that brother of yours won't step up, then we will. We can mind the store so you can have a nice little holiday some-where. Whatever needs doing the CWA sheilas have you covered. We're your mob, lovey."

Warmth flooded Maggie. Bless the old dears. They had merely wanted to offer their help (and gather as much gossip as possible!). Although images of the chaos they could cause if they were left in charge of the store was too horrendous to contemplate. Maggie's chest tightened as heartfelt emotions welled. "Thank you. Seriously, thank you. That is so kind of you."

The old ladies beamed back at her.

"Harrumph." Mrs. Gwozdek blinked rapidly behind her glasses and assisted Mary Porter to her feet. "We will now do our shopping," she stated in her ponderous tone.

With Aunty Deborah chomping on another chocolate bar, they made their way down the closest aisle, arguing in an amicable fashion with the ease of long-time friends.

Behind the counter, Maggie fingered the discarded wrappers reflecting on the old biddies' comments. In particular, she couldn't help wondering what was behind her parents' sudden decision to return home. Since their last phone call, worry had gnawed at the back of her mind. Then to receive that text from her brother which had been remarkably light on detail despite her repeated queries to her parents as well as Glen. Could ill-health be the reason they were heading home? Her parents had had a hard life to be sure. Running the store and trying to make a living in such a remote and small community would no doubt have taken its toll over the years. But neither of them had shown any obvious symptoms of illness before they'd set off in their motorhome. Now that she came to think of it, her mother had sounded definitely cagey in that last phone call – as if she was hiding something. If one of them was seriously ill...

Hands shaking, Maggie crumpled the wrappers and dropped them into a wastepaper basket.

A crash sounded from the rear of the store.

Aunty Deborah hollered, "Mary! I wish you'd watch where you're going with that thing. You are a menace on wheels! Just look at all that milk on the floor."

Maggie stood, burying her misgivings and worry for another time. She had a store to mind and judging by the commotion going on at the end of the aisle, one hell of a mess to clean up.

With a rueful smile, she picked up a mop and bucket.

CHAPTER
FIVE

Maggie cleared her throat and pushed back her tangle of red hair. She'd run a brush through the long strands but all she seemed to have achieved was a much wilder look than usual. "Hello. It's Maggie from *Living in the Outback* again. Today a very mysterious guy walked into the store."

Frowning a little, she pressed the pause button on her laptop stopping the recording while she thought about exactly what and how much she wanted to divulge to the *'world at large'* about her guest.

Weird how she felt reluctant to *'share'* him. It wasn't as if he was someone special, as if he meant anything to her. He was simply a bloke who happened to suddenly appear in her shop. Rolling her eyes, she growled a little as she slumped in her chair and glared at the ceiling fan whirling above her head.

This guy was a stranger. He certainly was easy on the eye and would hopefully attract more followers to her twice-weekly update on *Living in the Outback*. And more followers would be a Godsend considering how she currently had the lowly tally of forty-seven – the majority of whom were fellow Sturt Crossing townsfolk and her family.

When Snake had suggested she set up her own vlog in a bid to promote the region, Maggie had been sceptical. What would she say? Who would want to listen to her anyway? Her life was hardly interesting. She wasn't an Olympic Champion, she didn't scale mountains, invent amazing technology or surf the world's most dangerous waves.

No – she was small town Maggie Hayes.

A woman in her mid-thirties with no man (or a lover of any kind for that matter!) on the horizon. A woman who managed her parents' grocery store. Who lived alone with a small dog in a remote part of the world.

Put in raw terms it sounded pathetic. It was the life she'd chosen although there were days when she wondered what had happened to that teenager who'd dreamed she would spend her life exploring the world with little more than a backpack on her shoulders. Apart from a six-week Contiki tour through Europe when she was eighteen, she'd spent her entire life in Sturt's Crossing. The town was small, the population even smaller but she did have some lovely friends. She didn't see them as often as she'd like, given the huge distances that spanned the small towns and the rural properties in that part of the country. But the friends she did have, she knew she could count of them through thick and thin. They held similar interests to herself - loved to garden, were concerned about the environment, and loved to get together for a barbeque and catch up. Her life was full and interesting what with being a volunteer member of the town's rural fire brigade and the local Country Women's Association. Even during the *'off-fire'* season there was training once a fortnight and the CWA always had plenty of activities on the go. She'd never been one to sit and wait for life to happen. Her daily routine might sound boring to others, but she found being involved in the community extremely satisfying. It was only that sometimes – often when she lay alone in her bed - she yearned for more.

Straightening, Maggie pressed the button to begin the recording again. "So folks." She leaned closer to the screen to do an exaggerated eye roll and modulated her voice to a dramatic tone.

"Here's the thing. Is he or isn't he? We're desperate to find out the truth. Our livelihoods are at stake. Maybe our very lives! Everyone knows there is the possibility that gas fracking can have a horrendous impact on the water table. Sturt's Crossing lies in a very fragile environment. Many of us locals rely on bore water for our animals, our land, our produce. What will happen if our only water source becomes contaminated?"

She pressed the pause button and leaned back to consider her next words. Then nodding, she continued. "Enter one hot-looking guy who gives me a false name. I mean, who is called John Jones in real life? I'll tell you – it's not him. Which begs the question of not only – who is he – but why is he here?"

She stopped, deciding that here would be where she'd insert the photo she'd taken of her visitor with her mobile when he wasn't looking her way. It wasn't the best shot. A little out of focus and she'd only been able to capture him in profile. His Akubra had shaded a lot of his face. But his very nice physique would make a welcome change from her normal pics of local wildlife, flora and stunning sunsets. "This is our dilemma. One fake John Jones who may or may not be working for a mine company. If you know this man, drop me a line! And stay tuned for more developments as they happen in Sturt's Crossing."

Feeling pleased with her efforts, Maggie hummed as she played back the recording, deciding she hadn't come across too radical or feral-looking as she'd feared. Smiling, she set about up-loading the short film to her vlog before sending it out into the world.

A couple of hours later, the ham radio crackled to life.

Maggie snatched up the handpiece and muttered a vague, "Maggie, over." Since doing a tally of the register and checking the shelves for any products that would soon need restocking and after she'd recorded her latest session she'd become fixated on her vlog. She'd even shared it to her social media page. How exciting it was to see how many likes and shares her posts had received. She'd spent a few moments answering some of the comments and was debating whether she should do a follow up post or leave it for another day.

"It's Snake. What did you find out? Over."

"Nothing." With that single admission, some of her euphoria faded. She chewed her lip for a second before adding, "The bloke says his name is John Jones. And that he's just home from working in Antarctica! Huh! As if! Over."

"Damn, Maggie. Who cares what he's called? We need to know whether the rumour is true – that he's here to do tests on the viability of gas mining in our area."

Heat crawled over her face. She snapped, "Okay, okay. I did a vlog and included a photo of him. Over."

Silence.

Then, "Say again. Over."

"I did a vlog on him and uploaded a photo."

"Geeze....Maggie, are you asking for trouble? Did you get his consent? Over," squawked Snake in a voice so high pitched he could have auditioned for the opera.

Frowning, Maggie slumped in her chair. "Nope."

He blew out a gusty breath. "Well, let's hope the bloke isn't a fan of social media and doesn't see your post. Or if he does, isn't interested in suing you. Any thoughts about what we do next? Over."

Worry squirmed like wriggling worms in her belly. She pushed down on her anxiety and after a second or two of shuffling through her notebook, she muttered, "I've contacted the *'Shut the Gate'* group and they've given me a couple of phone numbers to call as well as a state minister's personal deets. I'm onto making those calls later this afternoon. Over."

"Sounds good. I'd hold off in plastering John's face and name over any more social media posts if I was you, Maggie. You coming to the pub, tonight? I've put the call out for another town planning meeting. Over."

"Yes, I'll be there about eight. Over."

"See you. Over and out."

Maggie set down the mic and looked up – straight into the furious face of Mr. John Jones.

"What gives you the right to post a photo of me on the net?" He waved his mobile an inch from Maggie's nose. "I have a right to my privacy and without the world knowing my whereabouts."

Oho. Seems Snake had been right. But it was too late now. All she could hope to do was soften any fallout. Trying to calm her shaking hands, she leaned back and raised an eyebrow. "Sounds like a man with something to hide."

"Don't be ridiculous. I'm simply a man wanting a little peace and quiet."

Oh how she wanted to make some snarky reply. But the problem was she probably *had* crossed a line and if she annoyed him too much he could well move out of the B&B and that was goodbye to her small commission. Time to soothe some oil on troubled waters and give herself another chance to discover exactly what he was doing in their town.

"Listen. It's nothing. I do a vlog now and then about living in a small town. You're the first visitor we've had in over thirteen weeks. I thought it was newsworthy." Maggie held her hands out, palm upwards and tried for warm and conciliatory. With no luck.

The expression on his face remained set and seriously pissed off. "Who was that you were just talking to? I specifically heard my name being mentioned."

"Only Snake. We chat sometimes throughout the day – it helps to pass the time." This time, she tried a friendly smile.

His scowl didn't budge as he glared back at her. He snapped his fingers. "I knew I'd seen you before. You've got that vlog about living in the Outback."

"Oh? You follow me?" Curiosity won over her feelings of being in the wrong.

He snorted. "Once or twice I might have caught a post when I had nothing better to do with my time."

The man really knew how to poke the bear. "Nice," Maggie drawled in a sarcastic tone. "How did you find out about the post?"

"A friend texted me."

"That was fast. My vlog only went on-line..." Maggie checked the time. "...about two hours ago."

A slight flush mounted on his cheekbones. "Yeah well. What can I say? Craig lives on the net. He was doing a bit of fishing for info about this area after I told him where I was staying. Curiosity and all that."

"Really? So you're not *that* adverse to having people know where you are."

He averted his eyes as his jaw worked.

She added when it appeared he wasn't going to respond. "Have you seen the video? What did you think?"

An impassive expression blanked his previous annoyance. "Very dramatic but I imagine that was the effect you were going for. As for all that emphasis on my mysteriousness – what a laugh. I told you – I'm on holiday."

"And that your name is John Jones," she shot back.

Mouth compressed, he glanced away. "It's my business if I want a little anonymity. Surely it's not too much to ask."

"What? So now you're some famous person? A movie star? No, wait. A member of the Royal family." She held back her laughter at his obvious chagrin.

"Now you're dreaming." His lips twitched.

"I'm not the one flying under false colours."

Sighing, he leaned against the counter, looking suddenly older. Tired. And was that sadness filling his dark eyes with shadows? "I don't understand why it's so important who I am."

Her amusement fled and more than ever she wished she'd never made the vlog. "Look, I'm sorry I mentioned you. You're right I should have asked permission to share your photo. All I can say is that using your sudden appearance in town was to try and stir up interest for our cause."

"What cause?"

"Then you didn't watch the film all the way through?"

He shook his head.

"Okay." Maggie picked up a folded camp chair and offered it to him. "Why not sit down for a spell? Here's the low down. There's been rumours flying around town the past few days about a mining company interested in drilling for gas in the area. We're concerned about gas fracking and the consequences to our environment by having mines in the area. The desert has a fragile eco system. Plus we're also worried about our water supply. We've heard about other towns impacted in an adverse way and want to head off any possible mine interest before it has a chance to get started."

Interest sparked in his eyes, and he leaned forward.

"Isn't there a lot of First Nation Land around here? The community elders will need to be consulted plus there'd need to be a ton of investigative reports and testing done which will have to be ratified by the government before the first shovel hits the dirt."

"There are three First Nation communities in our area and they are totally saying no to any mine going in here. But we're a long way from Canberra. We're hardly a huge population - the government probably doesn't even know where we are on the map. They may not be too concerned about a small bunch of people trying to scrape a living in the Outback. Or even on any deleterious impact to our land," Maggie said glumly. She knew she sounded negative, but she couldn't help voicing her concern over what might or could happen to the country she loved so much. "We need all the help we can get."

"Hence your internet post." He ran a hand through his hair then took a mouthful of water from the bottle he must have brought with him.

Seeing him drink, made Maggie remember her own bottle. She fished the brown glass out from under the counter and twisted off the cap, taking a deep swig. When she set the bottle down, she noticed how his eyes had narrowed, his mouth tight with disapproval. Now what had she done?

He leaned back in the camp chair, causing the old canvas to squeak. "I'm not here in a work capacity and I don't work for a gas mining company."

"You said you worked in Antarctica."

"True, but I'm a Station Communication Technical officer. That means I carry out maintenance on the

38

telecommunications systems in Mawson. I've been going there since my university days from April through to September, and I also sometimes do short stints at McMurdo Station over spring and summer. In fact, I've just come from McMurdo."

"But why the false name? I don't understand."

"It's personal." His jaw worked for a few seconds before he added, "Very well, since it looks like you're not going to give me any peace until you find out. My name is Jace."

"Jace Jones?" She smiled, tilting her head.

But he failed to respond, his face remaining stony. "Jace will do."

"Well, thank you for being honest. Jace. I'm Maggie." She held out her hand.

He gave her a brief shake, his touch leaving hers so fast she wondered whether he thought he might catch something if he lingered too long.

"We've had no Covid cases here for over six months," she said.

"After being away from civilisation for several months on the ice, I prefer to be a little cautious."

"Would you like me to take down the vlog?"

"No." Face carefully shuttered, he nodded then rose to his feet. After scooping up his water bottle, he walked out of the shop.

At least she had the right name to pin to his face. *Jace.* It suited him. Pity his candour had done little to alleviate his frostiness toward her. She would have loved to see his smile again.

But there was still the matter of the rumours. If Jace

was telling the truth that he wasn't the mine rep, then there remained the question of who the devil was. And secondly, how had whoever he or she might be, remained incognito for so long in such a small town.

Maggie pulled a pad and pen towards her. She listed the names of the town's inhabitants and anyone who'd had a guest or relative lodging with them recently. Then she made another list of the accommodation available in the area. The lists weren't that long. She laid the pen down with something of a snap. It shouldn't take too much time to check out every person and every site she'd written down.

Tomorrow she'd close the shop after the early morning *'rush'* was over and begin her sleuthing.

SIX

Dipping the brim of his Akubra against the glare of the broiling sun, Jace strolled along the main street. No point in walking at his usual brisk pace – not in that heat. Besides, it wasn't as if he had anywhere urgent to be. The idea of spending the remainder of his day holed up in his rented bedroom held little appeal. Nor did he feel like watching a mindless movie or TV show. Some exercise seemed to be just the ticket – even if he felt as if he was walking inside an oven.

A blue cattle dog was sprawled out the front of the butcher's shop. The dog yawned then gave himself an idle scratch behind his ear not even bothering to glance in Jace's direction as he approached. A paint-spattered elderly First Nations woman stood beside the dog peering into the shop window where a small selection of cut meats were displayed. She turned as if she'd heard his footsteps and a broad smile creased her brown face. "Gidday, young fella."

"Hey." Jace hesitated and stuffed his hands in his pocket. He didn't want to be rude and keep walking, but neither did he feel up to making polite conversation. Maybe he should have stayed in that bedroom after all.

"You gotta be that young gubba Maggie's got in her house."

"Jace." Amused at being called young, he held out his hand and found it clasped warmly.

The elderly lady stepped closer as if trying to see into his very soul. "You be good to her, you hear me, now?"

A flush scalded his skin.

"You can call me Aunty Deborah." She turned away and tapped a finger on the glass and raised her voice. "What do you reckon about that piece of beef? I think it's off. What we need is a health inspector." She sent Jace a cheeky wink.

The butcher burst out through the fly strips, a meat cleaver in his hand and a gory stained apron tied around his thick waist. "Aunty Deborah. What do you think you're doing? You're scaring away my customers."

Aunty Deborah erupted into a deep belly laugh. She clapped a hand hard on Jace's back. "This boy's no customer, Larry. He's got more sense than that. See you around, young fella." Still chuckling, she ambled down the road as if she had all the time in the world. She whistled. The cattle dog gave a mighty stretch, before trotting after her leaving Jace with the irate butcher.

"What can I help you with? How about some nice bacon? Or ham? I got a good porker in the other day." Larry beamed and rocked back on his bare feet. "Come in and have a better look." He cupped Jace by the elbow and gave a little shove.

Bowing to the inevitable Jace allowed himself to be manoeuvred inside the shop. Five minutes later he emerged rather bemused and clutching a small paper-wrapped package.

"Bloody highway robbery," he muttered as he continued on his voyage of discovery of Sturt's Crossing main street and ruminated over how much money he'd just handed over.

The concrete footpath merged into a hard packed earthen track the further down the road he went. He passed a building that had been a bank at one stage, its plate glass window boarded up by sheet iron and a massive lock on the front door. The white paintwork was smeared with a thin layer of red dust and weeds grew inside the thigh-high chain fence that separated the building from the wide road. The real estate office nearby was in a similar state but with cobwebs festooning the door handle. The pastoral care building had its windows shuttered and door shut tight but at least it didn't have the air of abandonment so many other buildings sported. At the next building, two sets of wooden tables and chairs were squished close against the glass wall of a gift shop that did quadruple duty as a café, newsagent and post office.

A sudden need to spend a few more dollars in what was obviously a dying town, hit him. He pushed open the screen door and found himself fronting a long counter where a few pastries and cakes sat on fine bone china plates. He leaned closer then grinned. The so-called food was made of plastic or he'd eat his hat.

Straightening, he looked around. A row of shelves on one wall showcased what were obviously locally made produce and homewares while the shop was divided by a half-wall down the centre where magazines, a couple of newspapers, various sized envelopes, postage packages, and greeting cards were stacked on both sides. On the opposite wall hung three oil paintings and five ink sketches along with an out-of-date calendar.

He stepped over to admire the pieces which were for sale, as noted by prices depicted on a small white card tucked into each frame. One in particular caught his fancy. It was of the nearby tors and painted after a rain shower as several rivulets of water washed down the face of a tor darkening its original colour. The bright splash of Sturt Desert Peas against the dusty-olive green greenery and the rich ochre of the tor with the stark blueness of sky above was striking. It would look perfect in his living room. Taking out his mobile he snapped a pic of the artist's details wondering whether the artist could have been Aunty Deborah. Hard to decipher the tiny inscription in the corner. He stepped back to the counter. It was quiet apart from the swish of the overhead fan and the hum of a refrigerator.

There appeared to be no one about so he pinged the bell next to the cash register.

A loud snort as if someone had just woken up, resounded from a doorway which led to another room, and he stifled his laugh. While he waited, he inspected the limited, handwritten menu printed on a laminated piece of cardboard.

A tall angular woman with short dark hair heavily shot with silver appeared. She wore a spotless white apron over a loose navy dress and had a pair of fire-engine red tennis shoes covering her feet. "Can I help you?"

The words were polite and friendly but there was no trace of a welcoming smile on her lined olive-skinned face.

"I'd like an iced coffee please and a Caesar salad wrap."

"Eat here or take away?"

"I'll eat outside."

She nodded and set about making his order. Once finished she placed the wrap onto a plate and pushed his coffee closer.

Jace paid, thanked her, and took his lunch outside where he sat under the shade of the awning and enjoyed his food. He'd just finished when a large fuel truck rumbled down the road, the only vehicle he'd seen since he'd stepped out of Maggie's shop. Shaking his head at how desolate the place appeared to be, he set off along the street once more.

The lots were wide and set far apart. Not every yard had a building, some lots were simply patches of dirt and straggling grass. Everywhere he looked, there was a proliferation of boulders, some large, some small enough to roll your ankle if you didn't keep a wary eye on the ground. Stunted trees grew where they could giving spotted shade and shelter from the blinding sun. With their drooping branches they were like bowed, defeated soldiers.

Most of the houses had wide verandas at the front, and garages or sheds made from iron. Several homes had bicycles out the front indicating that for all its small population, the town had a certain number of children. As if to reinforce that realisation a distant school bell peeled. Water tanks squatted at the side of every building – a reminder that even the tiniest drop of rain was precious.

At the far end of the street the large petrol station sign was a vivid bright blue, red and white against an endless sky so blue it hurt the eyes. When he'd arrived in town, he'd driven past a caravan park on the outskirts of town, but he didn't intend to walk that far – not in that heat.

Aware that his packet of bacon was becoming rather too warm in his sweaty hand, he changed direction and trudged along a gravel road until he found himself on Coolibah Street. It wasn't much longer, and he was mounting the front steps of the B&B, eager to be away from the heat.

Inside the house, Sherman was in his favourite armchair beneath the whirring air conditioner. The dog gave a half-hearted *'woof'* before returning to his slumber. After Jace placed the bacon in the refrigerator he poured himself a glass of ice water which he took into the living room. He joined Sherman, flopping onto the lounge and enjoyed the cool slide of liquid down his throat. The dog's eyes closed and soon the quiet room was filled with the animal's soft snores.

All those boarded up buildings had been downright depressing and his walk had done little to dispel the bitterness of his exchange with his mother. Maybe a little shut eye before dinner was just what Jace needed to settle his racing thoughts. About Douglas and his memorial. About his parents and the unread letter. Then there was his image being plastered all over the internet. Which led him to Maggie. Try as he might tell himself it was none of his business, he couldn't rid himself of her anxious expression when she told him about the possibility of a mine opening up in the area.

He placed the empty glass on a side table and pulling out his mobile he began to make notes.

CHAPTER
SEVEN

Night had fallen cooling the last remnants of the day's heat and overhead the dark sky was sprinkled with glittering stars like diamonds on black velvet. Red dust coated the straggling line of utes and four-wheel drives parked along the street. Maggie smiled as she recognised several vehicles. Seemed like Snake's *'call to arms'* had not gone unheeded with many of the surrounding station owners taking time off from their hard life on the land to attend the impromptu meeting.

Far too aware of the man who strolled by her side, she wriggled her shoulders a tad. "How was your dinner?" She herself had made do with a boiled egg and baked beans on toast after she'd fed Sherman. The thought of standing over a stove after such a hot day had not been very appealing.

"Surprisingly excellent. The chef knows how to cook."

"That's Egon. I heard on the grapevine that he's

worked in some of the finest restaurants all over the world."

"Which begs the question - what is he doing here?" Jace's tone was wry.

She shrugged as she said, "I guess he has his reasons." Ignoring the way her tummy turned to liquid every time his arm brushed against hers, Maggie pushed open the pub door and entered the main air-conditioned bar which hummed with noise and movement.

Welcome cool air blew onto her warm face. The whirl of ceiling fans competed with the hum of voices interspersed with shouts of laughter. Then the noise stopped as if chopped off with an axe as heads turned toward Jace.

"There he is! That's the fella. Come on, mates. Let's do him!" Larry Andrews, the only butcher in town, shot up from his chair like he'd been propelled by a cannon. Face infused with blood and probably a good deal of alcohol, he lunged across the room. His hands were outstretched as if he intended to grab Jace by the neck and throttle him where he stood.

At the very last second, Maggie pushed in front of Jace. Using all her strength she gave the butcher a mighty shove. Already three sheets to the wind, Larry flailed and went down like a domino in a tangle of chairs. The pub erupted into a frenzy of jeers, cat-calls and wild clapping.

Maggie tensed her muscles, ready for a repeat performance. "Geez, Larry. Get a grip, mate! This bloke isn't the mining rep."

Larry bounced back up, dancing on the balls of his feet. He held his hands in front of him and did a couple of wild air punches. "I can take him," he hollered which made Maggie burst into a fit of the giggles.

Old Charlie Mercer jumped to his feet and taking a boxer's stance, darted and weaved around Larry to the delight of the crowd. As usual, Charlie wore faded Army fatigues and boots so old his toes poked through the ends revealing a pair of lurid pink socks. A couple of the younger blokes smacked their beer glasses on the table to egg the prancing pair on.

"Just ignore them." Maggie headed to where a woman waved a hand madly in the air. She smiled. "Look, there's Rosie and Luke. I didn't realise they were coming into town tonight."

"Rosie, as in my landlady?" Jace followed her as she threaded her way through the maze of tables and chairs.

There were still plenty of empty chairs as it was a large room, the population of Sturt's Crossing and its surrounds wasn't particularly big in numbers. But it was heartening to see how many had turned up. It revealed more than words, how serious the community viewed the prospect of a mine in the area.

Grinning, Maggie stopped beside Rosie who leapt to her feet and gave her a hearty hug. Luke was more leisurely as he stood but his easy smile held nothing but a friendly welcome. Maggie sank into a spare seat. "This is Jace. Jace meet my best friend Rosie and her husband Luke."

After Jace had shook hands, he pulled up a chair next to her. "Quite a crowd." He took his time looking around the room while Rosie dug her sharp elbow into Maggie's ribs three times, accompanied by dramatic eye rolls.

When Maggie refused to take the bait, Rosie shifted a tad closer and said in what she believed to be a whisper, "What a honey. Where did you find him?"

Her cheeks burning, Maggie placed her elbows on the sticky table and hunched her shoulders. "He's staying at your B&B for a few days."

"Get out of here. Nothing like a little proximity to get things started."

"Nothing's starting." Maybe if she moved really fast she'd be able to strangle Rosie before she uttered another embarrassing word.

"Oh babe. You really need to get your skates on before someone else snaffles him."

Maggie huffed out an exasperated breath. "Like who?" The town was hardly bursting at the seams with single women.

Ignoring her, Rosie batted her lush lashes in Jace's direction. To his credit he gave the impression he hadn't heard her comments but Maggie detected how the tan over his cheekbones had deepened.

"Leave the bloke alone, Rosie." Grinning, Luke took a long pull of his beer then set the empty glass on the table. "Like a drink, mate?"

As if they were symbiotic twins, Jace and Luke surged to their feet. Jace placed his hand on the back of Maggie's chair. "Going to the bar. Would you like something, Maggie?"

"A cold beer would be great, thanks. Whatever Snake has on tap tonight will do."

No sooner had they wandered off, then Rosie shifted her chair closer. "Fess up and tell me everything." She laid dramatic emphasis on the word *'everything'*.

"There isn't anything to tell. He's a traveller. In a few days he will be gone."

Rosie slumped back in her chair, her lower lip forming a pout. "What a pity. You look so good together."

Time to deflect her bestie from a subject that was becoming quite confusing in her mind, Maggie said, "Your sister isn't here?"

"No, little Jim's got a bit of a cold and, you know how it is, Rach and Chris won't leave him until he's on the mend."

Maggie understood. These days any symptoms that bore even the slightest resemblance to those of Covid or Influenza were strictly monitored in the small town. They had to; being so far from a hospital and with no medical help for kilometres. Even in times of an emergency it could take the Royal Flying Doctor service a couple of hours to reach them. "I hope it's nothing too serious. Any other school kids with the same symptoms? And Milly is she okay?"

"Two other children in the same year as well as the new schoolteacher's daughter. Milly's fine so far."

They shared a concerned glance before Maggie said, "How's my godson? I was hoping he'd be here tonight so I could get some cuddles."

"Caleb is busy being spoiled rotten by George. I think Eleanor intended to drop by with a kid's DVD for them all to watch."

Drop by. Rosie managed to make it sound as if they

lived streets away instead of out on a sheep station a good five or so hours' drive from town. But that's what it took to stay in touch with friends out here.

"Sounds like fun." Maggie grinned. "Oh by the way, there's another guest arriving on Monday. A man called McKenzie. He's booked in for a minimum of a week."

"Nice. Keep 'em coming, Maggie. Any money is appreciated." Rosie grinned, displaying her dimples. "How long is Mr. Hot and Handsome staying?"

"He didn't say."

Rosie wiggled her eyebrows. "Sounds like he doesn't have anywhere he needs to get to in a hurry which means he may stay long enough to fall for you."

"Much good that will do me. He's not the type to live in a small town. What would he do for a living for starters?" Maggie folded her arms, sinking her chin down onto her chest. Funny how the thought of his leaving had dulled the shine off the evening.

"What does he do anyway?" Rosie took a long slurp of her drink.

"Something to do with communications. But get this – he works in Antarctica."

"No way." Then Rosie pinched Maggie's fingers. "Well, you always wanted to travel."

"Travel yes, but live somewhere else, no. My home is here." But even Maggie could hear the lack of conviction in her voice.

"Never say never. Shush, they're coming back."

Over near the bar, someone pounded a gong and the loud voices faded into silence as Luke and Jace returned to the table, beers in hands.

Jace placed Maggie's glass down and slid into his chair. "What's going on?"

"The town meeting about the gas company is about to start." Maggie chugged down the amber beverage, the liquid flowing easily down her throat until her glass was empty. It tasted too good. The frown on Jace's face when he stared at her empty schooner glass, reminded her of how easy it was to fall into the habit of drinking to soften the harsh realities of life in the Outback. Hadn't she witnessed the pattern too often herself?

There had been her high-school friend Sally who had wrapped her car around a telegraph pole when coming home from a night out doing pub crawls in Walgett. Poor Sally. Her boyfriend had dumped her to take off for the bright lights of the city and an easier life. She'd been devastated. She'd thought – they had all thought – that theirs was a relationship that would weather time. The crash had left Sally in a wheelchair and living on welfare with her single mother, and they had moved soon after to the Eastern coast. Closer to better medical facilities. The police investigation into the cause had revealed her alcohol limit had been off the charts. One bad decision had completely changed her life.

With a sickening lurch of her belly, Maggie realised it had been a good three years since they'd exchanged any kind of contact – and even then, it had been nothing more than a simple text message. Anything could have happened.

The taste of the beer on Maggie's tongue turned sour and she instantly resolved to reach out to Sally the very next day. She pushed the half-empty glass a little away from her and twisted around to face the bar.

Snake raised both hands in the air. "First off, I wanna thank each and every one of ya for being here tonight. I know it was a big ask, but if a gas mine commences operation in the area, that will impact all of us."

Francesca Stillman who owned and ran the small newsagent cum post office cum gift shop and cafe, rose to her feet. Her expression was stern as she swept her gaze around the room. "What about the money that a mine will bring to the community? Has everyone here truly thought through our intention to oppose a mine operation?"

Several people thumped their tables while others shouted her down until Snake hammered on the bar counter with his meaty fists.

"Pipe down you lot!" he roared, waiting until the room subsided. "No one is denying this town needs money. It needs people, better services. Hell, it needs just about everything. But we also need a future for ourselves and our kids."

Rosie bellowed, "We've got plans to put this place on the map. Tourist dollars – that's where our future lies!"

A wild burst of clapping erupted drowning out Mrs. Stillman's response.

Mouth pinched tight Mrs. Stillman subsided in her chair.

"What's the latest?" Aunty Deborah stood next. "I'm here as a representative of the council elders. Our mob is worried. We don't want any mines destroying our country."

"None of us do, Aunty Deborah." Snake leaned back against the bar. "Were you able to get that petition signed?"

Aunty Deborah raised a sheet of paper. "No worries, mate."

A round of applause swept the room.

"Give it to me after the meeting." Snake lifted a notebook from the counter and paused as he riffled through the pages. He cleared his throat. "Okay, so we've got a few proactive actions we can take. If anyone here knows a MP or someone with clout, come and see me afterwards. Maggie's got the name of one or two who may help but the more social noise we can stir up the better. We need public opinion on our side. That's the only way to sway the politicians in our favour."

"Has a geological survey already been carried out? And what about an environmental impact study? If it's gotten this far, then sample drilling would have been carried out in the area – the results of which should be included in their proposal. If you can nab a copy this will give you a better opportunity to line up your objections and correlate a sound legal argument. Have you contacted the media newspaper, tv networks? I reckon Current Affairs might be interested to investigate. And one of those morning shows might host a segment," Jace called out.

A low murmur of voices flowed through the room and several people craned their necks to get a better look at the stranger in town who'd joined the conversation.

Snake nodded slowly. "That's who we've been trying

to get interested in our issue but so far none of the nobs we've contacted are returning our calls."

"I may be able to help. My father's got some connections..." Jace hesitated as tiny beads of sweat formed on his forehead, then cleared his throat. "Well, give me a list of names and I'll see what I can do."

Was it Maggie's imagination or had he gone a trifle pale?

A round of applause thundered through the room then Snake raised his voice again. "Excellent, thanks mate. Alright you lot, bring over your suggestions and we'll divvy up the work. Drink up but don't forget you can kip down in the bar if you're over the limit." He flapped his notebook about in the air then pointed to where Senior Constable Anderson was enjoying his dinner at a table near the restaurant area.

Lou Botha, who with his wife and small family was a recent refugee immigrant from South Africa, raised his empty glass and hollered, "Does dat mean drinks are on da house?"

Everyone roared with laughter while Snake spluttered out a denial.

When the bedlam had settled somewhat, Maggie eyed Jace thoughtfully.

What was behind his gesture – a genuine desire to help out? Or could he be that rep afterall? Maybe he wanted to suss out exactly where they were up to in their efforts to dissuade the mining company? But if it was the latter, that would mean that he was in cahoots and up to his rather handsome neck with the mining company and that thought didn't sit well in Maggie's mind. She wanted him to be exactly what he said he was – a traveller passing through with no hidden agenda. Or even better a traveller who decided Sturt's Crossing held more than one attraction to make him want to stay.

An elbow jabbed her ribs jerked her from her fantasy. She looked up into Rosie's sparkling eyes and mischievous smile. Maggie sighed inwardly. Marriage certainly agreed with her bestie and since she'd tied the knot with Luke, she was always dreaming up ways and means for Maggie to join her in wedded bliss. But much as Rosie wanted Maggie to be happy, she also didn't want her to settle for anyone less than what she was worth – as she so often told her. And as for Maggie? Well, she wanted the kind of relationship her parents' had – one that could power through all that life sometimes threw at you.

"That was kind to offer your help," she said to Jace.

Jace shrugged. "No biggie. It won't take me long to make a few phone calls. Sounds like you could use some assistance that won't involve plastering my name and face all over your social media pages."

She ducked her head and picked at the cardboard coaster. "I can remove the vlog."

"Huh? What did I miss?" Rosie sat up straighter, her gaze snagging Maggie's.

"Nothing really." She tried to laugh her blunder off.

But placing his elbows onto the table, Jace leaned forward. "Maggie did a vlog referring to me as a mystery man and asking the public for information about me."

"No!" Rosie snapped shut her mouth. "And did they?"

"I haven't checked for any responses. I've been busy."

Liar. She'd barely torn her gaze from the screen all afternoon. Maggie locked her fingers together. The coaster had been reduced to shreds of paper.

But her friend wasn't impressed. "Busy? Doing what?"

"Working. I have a shop to run." Maggie glared around the table as Rosie hooted and Luke chuckled.

Even Jace appeared amused, a smile glinting in his blue eyes.

"Oh, I get it – payback time." She sank back against the chair.

"Only a little." And he grinned.

Laughing, Maggie lifted her hands in the air. "I can take it down if you really want me to?"

"Let's forget it and move on." The words might have been curt, but both his voice and the accompanying smile told her he harboured no long-standing grudge over her actions. Turning to Luke, he asked, "What type of work do you do?"

Luke plunged into a narrative about the family sheep station and how it was morphing into camel farming as well as the tourism enterprise they operated.

Jace listened, inserting a question here and there and sounding genuinely interested. "So the tour is a cross between a treasure hunt and a scavenger hunt?"

Luke grinned. "Yeah, dreamed up by my babe here and my brother. Clues to be solved along with an outback adventure tour. It runs over seven days, and everyone winds up with a chance to mine for their own opals."

"What's the treasure?" Jace leaned forward eagerly.

"The long, lost and legendary Bloodwood gold nugget." Rosie giggled as she answered. "Of course, its fake and we tell everyone that straight up so there's no confusion. The tours are targeted at the eighteen- to forty-year-olds. We trace Sturt's footsteps on camels and the clues are hidden at each location we stop." She snuggled into her husband's side. He sent such a heated and fond look at her, before returning to his conversation with Jace, that Maggie felt a tug on her heartstrings.

Dimly, she was aware of Jace peppering Luke with more questions as her thoughts turned inward. What she wouldn't do to have a man – not just any man but a good and kind man – give her such a glance. One that told her and the world that she was the only woman for him. And then of course there was the wonderful prospect of children. Rosie and Luke already had little William from Rosie's first marriage and Luke loved him as if he was his own son. She had hinted several times lately, that they had decided to try for another baby.

The need to hold a baby of her own in Maggie's arms, was an ever-present ache these days. No one was more aware of the passing of time than her. The years seemed to fly by and she'd already passed her thirty-fifth birthday. She hugged her waist, feeling her empty womb beneath her fingers.

The problem was and always had been that there weren't many options in a region as small as Sturt's Crossing. Most of the eligible blokes in the area had been snapped up and although she was fond of the remaining inhabitants, she drew the line at a husband so old he had no teeth.

Or one that preferred the bottom of his beer glass than being with his wife or girlfriend and unfortunately there were quite a few of those types in town. Anyway being the full-time manager of her parents' shop meant no holidays, no trips into any larger nearby towns that could broaden her opportunities. Her hopes and dreams for a family of her own would have to wait a little longer.

"Penny for your thoughts?" Jace shoulder nudged her.

Maggie looked up straight into his intense eyes and smiling mouth. Her tummy lurched. All of a sudden, she had the awful thought she was about to burst into tears. Something in her expression must have warned him her thoughts were unhappy because he frowned, his lips turning down.

She rushed into speech with the first thing that popped into her mind. "I was wondering whether you've seen Blackbird Tor? We could go for a camel ride and picnic near the opal mine." Damn. Had that come off as too obvious?

"Camels?" Jace grinned showing slightly crooked but lovely white, well cared-for teeth.

He has his own teeth. Maggie bit down on the absurd desire to giggle at her earlier thought.

"Yes." Rosie shared a smiling glance with her husband. "Our Outback Mystery Adventure tour business includes camel riding. It's a pity we were only just getting it off the ground when Covid hit. We've only just started up again although bookings have been a bit slow." She snapped her fingers. "I know. Why don't you both join the tour that's currently running? We have glam tents and they're very comfortable. On the house - because we're friends and the tour is almost at the end."

That telling heat sizzled over Maggie's cheeks again as Rosie pinned her down with her bright-eyed stare while everyone waited for her and Jace's response. Her blush deepened as the seconds ticked by and he didn't speak. How embarrassing if he didn't want to spend any time with her.

Luke inserted, "That's a great idea. I can organise with Mason for you to drive out to a designated meeting place."

"Sounds like a plan. I'm in." Jace chinked his glass against Luke's. "When can you get time off from the store, Maggie?"

"Um." Her mind went blank while she stressed over whether he really wanted to go or whether her friends as well as herself had backed him into a corner and he'd felt he had no choice.

Rosie prodded her. "It has to be soon though before your parents return. You'll probably want to spend time with them before they leave again."

"When are they due back? For some reason I got the impression they lived in New South Wales." Jace turned towards Maggie.

She wiggled on the chair. "They're travelling around Australia in one of those large motorhomes. They started their retirement with a cruise to Fiji before they bought the RV. They've been on the road a couple of years now. Last time we spoke they were staying at Nelsons Bay in Port Stephens. When the lockdowns occurred, they spent months camping near Longreach." How much should she share with a virtual stranger? Maybe it didn't matter what she divulged; her parents' lives were hardly state secrets. But still – she didn't know this bloke from Adam and she wasn't one to open up to a relative stranger – regardless of how attractive he was. "They're due home next week. I'm not sure how long they intend to stay here though. They've been a bit short on details. My brother Glen is going to text me the exact day once the specifics have been finalised."

Rosie flung her arms around Maggie's shoulders and hugged her hard. "Then, that's settled. Let's organise it for this weekend before your parents get here and you'll be busy catching up with them. I'll mind the store so you can't use that as an excuse. You and Jace are going to have fun!"

Maggie emerged from Rosie's embrace, flushed and feeling giddy with a mixture of excitement and trepidation. "Separate tents, of course." She peeped over to find Jace's gaze settled on her face.

"Of course," he agreed. "Wouldn't have it any other way."

And just like that, every sizzle of excitement Maggie felt was effectively snuffed out like a candle in a thunderstorm.

EIGHT

The next day, Maggie shut up the shop for a couple of hours, after deciding no more customers were likely to brave the fierce sun until the heat had eased somewhat. From under the counter she took out a blue folder with several tabs separating each section. Since she would be walking about the town, she may as well do her rostered checks on the vulnerable and elderly – one of the activities the CWA had undertaken. When the doctor from Walgett turned up each month, the notes would be copied and handed over for review. This week it was Maggie's turn to undertake the health check.

She shoved a blank notebook, a full bottle of water and her mobile into a small backpack which she slung over her shoulders. After shrugging into a long-sleeve cotton shirt to shelter her bare arms from burning, she popped a pen into the breast pocket, plonked her hat onto her head and closed the shop door. With a nod, she taped the note advising when she would re-open onto the frame.

Operation *'sniffing out the enemy'* had begun.

Slipping on her sunnies, she paused on the footpath and examined the main street. While she'd attended to the few shoppers over the course of the morning, she'd mapped out a plan of attack which basically equated to knocking on every door in town. Since several buildings were boarded up and abandoned, that action shouldn't take more than a few hours allowing for some rests in the shade here and there. But people in Sturt's Crossing liked a chat and now that she really thought about it, checking each house and store could well take her the remainder of the day. She dithered a moment and unfolded the mud map she'd sketched earlier and planned out the route she intended to take. The main street first then she'd scour the east side of the small town before heading over to the few streets and properties that lay to the west. There were also a small number of houses on larger acre lots on the outskirts but no way did she intend to walk that distance. Maybe she could ask Jace for his company and the use of his air-conditioned car. Hers was a jeep so old it could have seen service in the last world war. Hot vinyl seats and no air con. Walking was preferable.

Tipping her hat lower, she set off. With limited recreational outlets, the occupants along the main road were all home. But Maggie's progress was slow going. Everyone invited her inside out of the heat. Everyone wanted to press a cool glass of water on her. And everyone wanted a gossip – the main topic being the handsome stranger. So far, no one had noticed anyone else who was new to town.

When she came to the last intersection, she walked east, her steps not quite so jaunty as when she'd started out what with the heavy heat weighing her down. Her phone pinged. Upon opening her messages, she smiled. First thing that morning, she'd attempted to contact her old school friend, Sally but her call had gone through to voice mail. Now she read the text eagerly. It seemed Sally had been at the local pool with her physio and was excited to hear from her. Maggie texted back, saying that she'd call again later in the afternoon.

A car pulled up beside her making her jump.

There was the whir of an electric window and Jace leaned over the passenger side. "Hop in."

Maggie didn't need to be told twice. She scrambled inside and lowered her hot face to the vent where blessedly cool air blasted. "Oooh that is lovely. Thanks. Give me a few minutes to cool down and I'll be out of your hair."

"No worries. Listen." Jace raked a hand across his jaw, the expression on his face radiating concern. "It's far too hot to be walking about outside. I take it, you're doing a tad of detective work looking for that mine rep? Why don't I drive while you do the door knocking?"

"I couldn't ask you to do that – aren't you on holiday?"

"You didn't ask, I offered." He shrugged. "Besides, I did offer my services last night."

What a pity it was only in relation to the town's

threat. She told herself to behave as he added, "How far have you got?"

She gave a rueful smile. "I've only done the main road."

"It will be faster my way."

"OK, thanks. I do appreciate it." She slumped back against the seat and tapped a finger against the map. "So far, I've found no strangers, or visiting family members or friends from out of town."

"What makes you think it's a stranger? Does it have to be someone you don't know?" Jace adjusted the air con to full-bore.

"What? You think it's one of us?"

"Why not? The butcher is a bit volatile. He gave the appearance of a man desperate for trade. And that post office lady - last night she made it obvious she is pro mine."

"I've known Mrs. Stillman all my life!" spluttered Maggie.

"We all have two faces." He turned his own face away from her as he spoke. "No disrespect but I imagine the offer of some easy money would be hard to say no to – this town doesn't strike me as one rolling in the dosh."

"That's a horrible thought. And I don't buy it – no one here has the knowledge to run any kind of tests or whatever the mining company needs."

"Probably not but they could quite easily obtain soil and rock samples for example from different areas, label them up then deliver or mail them somewhere else. Maybe what you should also be looking for, is someone who is splashing about a bit more cash than usual. Or someone who has a new car. Maybe even check the post office to see who has been mailing a lot of parcels recently. That kind of thing. Although if it is your Mrs. Stillman she's hardly going to fess up."

Maggie stared down at her hands in her lap. "I don't like the idea of spying on my neighbours. I know everyone in this town. It's hard to imagine anyone working against the rest of us."

"Money does strange things to all of us. Someone could need that money badly. Everyone has secrets."

"Like you?"

Turning to face her, he nudged her chin with his knuckle and grinned. "Good one. I didn't see that coming."

"It was worth a try." She smiled.

"My life isn't so much a suspicious secret, rather I value my privacy. I'm not one for sharing or getting too close to others."

Was that a warning? Her spine stiffening, Maggie compressed her lips. Well, she wasn't that desperate for a man of her own that she'd throw herself on someone who obviously wasn't interested. She did have *some* pride. Her voice considerably colder than previously, she said, "The closest two houses on this street are empty. If you could drive a little further on, that would be appreciated."

"I've said something to offend you. That wasn't my intention," Jace admitted as he set the car into motion.

He was fishing but she had no intention of divulging her attraction for him and certainly not after that his *I don't get too close* comment! The sedan rolled down the gravel road with a quiet hum of its engine.

"Is your car electric?" Interest sparked and Maggie leaned closer to inspect the dashboard.

"Hybrid and it's a hire car. Bit pointless having my own when I'm away for a good chunk of the year. But in saying that, I can't wait until there are charging stations all over the country. I believe it's the direction everyone has to take, or the consequences will be dire for our planet."

"Me too."

Their gazes locked.

Maggie's heart thumped slow and hard against her ribs as the moment stretched on until Jace frowned and jerked his head away. His fingers drummed on the steering wheel while Maggie willed the unwelcome flush from her face.

She folded the map, the rustle of paper the only sound in the quietness of the cabin. Then finally she said, "Pull over here, please. The next lot of houses are reasonably close together. Why don't you drive on and I'll meet you further up the road?"

But Jace switched the engine off. "How about I come with?"

"It will be slower. Everyone is curious about the new guy in town."

"Exactly. Meaning they'll be more open to a long conversation, and you never know someone may slip up. Come on." He slid out of the car, keys in hand.

Maggie succumbed to the temptation to spend more time with him. With a bounce in her step, she joined him on the road. So what if he was only passing through? An hour or two with an attractive man didn't mean she would fall for him – that idea was completely absurd.

As she suspected, the east side of town had yielded no results and the day was marching on what with everyone wanting to grill the man by her side. She blushed a little as she recalled some of the very pointed questions; *married? Children? Oooh – single are you. How long will you be staying?* Accompanied with a lot of nodding and significant glances towards Maggie.

Jace had endured the nosiness with composure and had competently deflected the subject every time. Shaking off her embarrassment, Maggie checked the time, thinking about the note left on the shop door. She'd give it another half an hour then she'd have to return to the store. Maggie directed Jace over to the scattered houses west of the main street and to a parking spot beneath a low-growing mulga which had a wide canopy. "We can leave the car here under the shade while we walk the rest of the way."

"No worries."

Akubra on his dark hair he soon joined her where she waited beside the car, enjoying the temperature drop afforded by the tree. "What we need is more trees," Jace mused as he peered at the branches above his head.

"And the water so they will survive." Maggie sighed and fanned herself with the map in her hand. "There's the *20 Million Trees* program run by the government, plus a number of private businesses that focus on planting trees like *Greenfleet*. It would be good if we could see more being planted in the desert regions."

"Water is the key to everything. Unfortunately, we have no idea how much groundwater lies in the water tables. And if these massive, long-term droughts continue to occur the future of our nation could be in serious trouble."

"I agree." Maggie set off down the road, walking and talking. "We've already had rural towns that have run out of water and seen water restrictions implemented all over the country. It's a growing problem."

"I see I've met a fellow environmentalist." He flashed a grin in her direction.

Despite her best efforts to quell her reaction, a warm glow spread beneath her breasts. "I try to mix my enthusiasm with common sense. We have a country to feed and an economy that has to be kept healthy."

"I believe there are ways we can work together to achieve a positive outcome for everyone."

"Really?" She narrowed her eyes.

He nodded as he opened a rusty gate and waved her through. "I've been thinking for some time that a change in career is on the cards and working for either the government or a business focussed on alternative renewable energy would give me a lot more job satisfaction."

"Then why don't you?" Maggie shrugged as she stepped onto the front porch and knocked on the door.

"You make it sound so easy."

"Isn't it? You're single, no apparent ties so nothing is holding you back."

Jace shifted his feet causing the old boards beneath his boots to creak. "You don't mince your words."

"It's too hot to flaff about a subject. I like to get straight to the point." She grinned. "Brace yourself, if you think I'm direct, wait until you meet Aunty Deborah."

Footsteps approached and then the door swung open. Aunty Deborah stood in the hallway, a big smile brightening her dark face. "Well, if it isn't our Maggie with the gubba from the butcher shop. Come on in."

"You've met?" Maggie shot Jace a look, as she entered the house.

"Briefly." He smiled and greeted the elderly woman.

They followed Aunty Deborah along the dim hallway until it opened out into a large, rectangular room at the rear of the house. At one end of the room was a kitchen and the remainder was obviously an artist's studio. An air-conditioner unit droned away on one wall. Two easels were set up near the centre of the room beside a table which was covered with brushes, tubes of paint, jars of water and paint-stained rags. A sketch book was opened revealing a charcoal drawing. Completed paintings were stacked in racks lining the full length of the room along with piles of blank canvases of all sizes.

An old blue heeler dozed on a rug. He lifted his head to eyeball them before falling back asleep.

Aunty Deborah picked up a paint brush and stood in front of the painting she was working on. After popping a lolly from the pile on the counter into her mouth, she sucked with gusto. "There's cold water in the fridge. Help yourself." Her offer came out rather mumbled.

"This is beautiful." Jace crossed immediately to the other easel to admire the painting resting there.

"That's kind of you to say so, young fella."

"I mean it." Jace pushed his hands to his hips and gazed around the room. "Do you sell any of these? I know a bloke in Melbourne who I'm sure would love to sell these for you on commission."

Maggie placed her backpack against the refrigerator and got out three glasses from the cupboard. She opened the fridge and poured out some cold water for everyone. "That's all taken care of. We've got a shop website set up."

"Still – a public viewing of your work could do wonders for your career."

Aunty Deborah leaned closer to her painting and squinted, "Don't like cities."

"I guess you may not need to appear in person. You could have someone you trust represent you."

She shrugged and added a daub of paint.

It appeared Jace intended to pursue the subject but before he could utter another word, Maggie's phone rang.

"Excuse me." A little surprised, she located the shrilling phone in her backpack and walked down the hall to answer. "Hello? Maggie speaking."

"Sis? Is that you? Thought it was time I gave you an update about Mum and Dad. Now – don't panic."

Words that immediately spiralled her into just that state! Her heart stuttered. "Glen – what's going on? Where are you? Why hasn't anyone been answering my calls and texts?"

"In Newie...sis, ...it's Dad. He's in hospital."

Maggie sagged against the wall while all kinds of horrendous possibilities roared through her head. Her brother continued to speak but all she could make out were the words... "three weeks...operation..."

An operation! What exactly was wrong?

Sweat broke out over suddenly clammy skin and she had to tighten her grip on the phone, or it would have fallen through her shaking fingers. "What? Glen, this connection sucks. I didn't hear you. Can you repeat what you just said."

The line cleared. "Sorry, sis. I'm in the hospital carpark and I'm almost out of juice. I'll call again later."

Then radio silence as the connection was lost.

CHAPTER
NINE

E xactly what had he gotten himself into? When he'd decided to avoid his family reunion and lose himself in a remote part of the world, no way had Jace factored into the equation spending time with a woman he found far too attractive. Yet somehow he'd agreed to venture into the back of beyond on a camel of all things!

Still – he couldn't deny how his spirits had risen at the very idea of camping with Maggie by his side. The experience sounded like an adventure. And the possibility he might come across the area where he, Doug and his father had holidayed so many years ago was another temptation he couldn't resist. The memories of those days were hazy at best, but they were enveloped in a warm fuzzy feeling he felt compelled to seek out and attempt to re-live.

He stepped out of the house to be met by a wall of heat like a physical force pushing against him. Hurriedly he checked the front seat of his car for his hat and sunnies then took a moment to admire the sunrise.

Dawn was a spilled jewellery box of red, orange and gold painted across the eastern sky as Jace waited beside his hire car, overnight holdall packed and already stashed in the boot. He resisted the urge to pace. If Maggie had changed her mind about going, she would have let him know last night. He had nothing to be worried about – still, he couldn't help but recall that phone call the previous day and wonder whether she'd received any more news from her family.

A part of him was still antsy, wondering what the hell he was doing spending an entire weekend in the company of a woman he'd never see again once he left town. But another part, and it was a much bigger part, had his pulse racing and his body tingling. Bloody hell, it had been too long since he'd been in the company of an attractive woman. Maybe he should think about culti-vating a long-term relationship – like a girlfriend. It would be good to have someone to come home to – the crazy thought stopped his jingling of the keys in his hand. Was it the town with its close-knit community vibe making him re-evaluate his life? Or Maggie herself? Or maybe it was the realisation of exactly how long he'd been alone.

The door whirled open and there she stood. Her hair like liquid flames licking over her shoulders and framing an open face with eyes that sparkled like the deepest forests. Something crackled to life between them. For the life of him, he couldn't stop himself from bounding forward and taking the handle of the wheeled luggage bag from her hand.

"Good morning." His blood pumped thick and hard, and he gave into the urge he'd battled since the first moment he laid eyes on her. He leaned forward and touched his lips to hers.

Her eyes widened. She caught her breath. A tiny sound that for some reason, sent his imagination into overdrive.

He slid his mouth over her soft contours and their lips fused. The bag fell from his fingers as he glided his hands around her waist, pulling her close. The moment her body pushed against his, the surge of heady desire thrummed through his veins with a ferocity that startled him. Utilising every atom of will-power, he forced himself to step away. His breathing came quick and heavy, his only consolation over his loss of control was that she appeared to be equally affected. A flush had formed over her cheeks and heat glowed in her lovely green eyes.

"Wow. Now that's what I call a good morning." Her smile was so warm and welcoming, he all but fell into it.

Jace fisted his hands. "Sorry, I didn't mean…" What did he mean? How could he explain his actions to her when he had no idea what he'd been thinking? The issue was, he hadn't been thinking, he had allowed some kind of crazy primal instinct to take control. Hell – would she think he intended this to be a dirty weekend? Fire flared over his face as he shuffled his feet.

Sherman provided a heart-felt distraction as he

trotted over to join them, plopping onto the ground with a goofy grin on his face.

"Hello boy." Jace crouched and fondled the little dog's ears, receiving a barrage of frantic licks in return accompanied by the furious wagging of his tail.

"I don't want to leave him by himself all weekend. Do you mind if he comes with us?" Maggie's cool voice helped Jace to regain his composure.

"Of course not. I used to have a dog myself once." He stopped, astounded that he'd allowed that snippet about his past to escape.

But Maggie didn't seem to notice or if she did, she was kind enough not to make a big deal about it. Instead, she wheeled her luggage to the car where she turned around and gave a dramatic eye roll. "I know this looks like I'm going for a month, but it contains Sherman's food, his bed and his favourite stuffed toy."

Jace grinned as the awkward moment vanished. He scooped the little guy up into his arms and placed him onto the back seat, his earlier anticipation returning full-fold. "Not a problem. We can't have this fella feeling homesick, now can we? Come on, let's get under way."

A few minutes later and Sturt Crossing was a speck in his dusty rear window. "Have you heard from your parents or your brother?"

"Another text message saying everyone was doing okay. Pretty brief. But that's Glen all over. The worst communicator in the world. He either mislays his mobile or seems to forget he has a sister and parents." She sounded resigned but no sign of tears. Or despair.

Hopefully that meant her father's stay in hospital wasn't serious. After that abrupt phone call yesterday, Maggie had aborted their mission to uncover the mystery mine rep and had hurried back to the store muttering something about *'getting everything ready'*. He had had dinner at the pub and when he'd returned to the house her bedroom door was firmly shut. He'd taken the hint. Spent a couple of hours star gazing and thinking about that damn, unread letter before heading to bed himself. While he was nutting over whether he should push and ask, she surged into speech.

"The news could have been worse, which is a blessing. I finally got through to Mum via the hospital. Apparently, Dad had climbed the ladder onto the roof of their RV when he slipped and fell. He broke his hip and dislocated his right shoulder and knee; hence the surgery to put him back together again." She sent him a rueful smile. "Mum had a panic attack and had to be hospitalised herself. And then there was Dad's rehabilitation after the operation which is why I hadn't heard from her. She assumed Glen had called and given me all the details. And Glen being Glen didn't – until yesterday. It would have been nice to have been included in the loop. All I'd been told was that they were returning home."

Her voice was quiet, even a little bleak as she added, "Glen would have been contacted almost immediately so he could organise driving their RV back. According to my father only men are capable of handling such difficult vehicles."

Jace reached over and squeezed her fingers. "Could

have been worse. So, your father's coming back to recover. Do you think they'll continue travelling once he's on his feet?"

"No idea. They were living their retirement dream. I don't know if they have a plan B."

He frowned as he mulled over her words and the underlying emotion. He slowed down to a crawl so they could navigate around the road gang.

"It's gravel and bull dust from here on in," Maggie said waving to the workers as they passed.

Jace also smiled, dipping his head at the chick holding the *'slow'* lollypop sign. At least he assumed she was female from the length of hair hanging down her back. Hard to tell for certain though with all the protective clothing, hat and cloth mask she wore.

From the back seat, Sherman whined. Maggie turned around and lifted him onto her lap. "Tell me about working in Antarctica. What made you decide to go there?"

He could feel her gaze boring into him and shifted a little on the seat. "It's always fascinated me as a kid. All that ice. I wanted to see first-hand Orca and Blue whales, penguins and the fur seals. Experience living in a place that's so different to where I grew up." He paused, his mind travelling through time to when both he and Doug had spent hours discussing and pouring over research on the vast southern continent. "It was both my brother's and my dream to go there. When he died, I felt that I couldn't not go. Check it out for both of us." A little stunned that he'd shared this treasured memory, he fell silent.

"I'm sorry about your brother." Her voice was quiet. Warm. Comforting.

He soaked it up, feeling her empathy wrapping around his lonely heart. "Thanks. It was a long time ago," he muttered.

Instead of probing a wound that had never fully healed, she said, "Tell me about the first time you went to Antarctica. Was the ice everything you imagined?"

"Hell yeah. Better in fact." A grin spread over his face, chasing the shadows from his mind. "I love it."

She laughed. "You must. If you still continue to work there."

He met her gaze. "You'd love it, too. There's this silence, a curious stillness. A bit like the Outback actually. Ever thought about travelling? Or living somewhere else?"

"All the time," she admitted, the smile vanishing from her face and leaving a seriousness that revealed more than one regret. "I keep telling myself that soon, next year, I'll do something about it. I told myself there was plenty of time."

"And now?"

"I'm thirty-five," she blurted.

He gave a mock gasp. "You'll be drawing your old-age pension next."

"Funny." She grinned.

"Thirty-nine in January for me."

"I'm surprised you don't have your electric mobility chair by now."

He laughed.

Maggie began to worry a fingernail and added slowly

in a wondering tone, "After high school, I had a holiday in Europe. Then there were a couple of trips to the coast about a decade ago. I can't believe it's been that long."

"What kept you here?" He had a pretty good idea what *had*; but he asked anyway.

She shrugged. "Not sure really. I guess I became too comfortable and then I always felt that my parents expected me to be the reliable one and take over from them. Glen was never around. He works as a shearer, a drover, a jackaroo – always conveniently far from Sturt's Crossing. He even picks fruit during harvest season. Anything to do with being on the land and away from cities. When he took off after he finished school, I felt that I couldn't desert them too."

"Have you spoken to your parents about finding your own path?"

"That's one discussion we've never had," she said slowly. She thought of Sally and their phone call the previous night and her old friend's surprise when she heard Maggie still lived in Sturt's Crossing. Although confined to a wheelchair, Sally had taken two cruises and three trips to New Zealand. She had confided that she swam twice a week and was a member of a local bush-walking group that catered for people with disabilities. Apparently they had an excursion almost every other week. Such a stark contrast to Maggie's life of minding the store and meeting friends at the pub once a month – if then.

"You know this could be your chance while your father recuperates. Think about what you want to do with the next stage of your life. It doesn't have to be forever. You can always come home. But if you want something different, you need to do something about it or one day you'll wake up to find yourself still here and you *will* be drawing that pension."

TEN

S herman snored as he slept on Maggie's lap, his claws digging for a second into her thigh. Without waking the little dog, Maggie shifted position and stared at the passing landscape. A heat mirage shimmered in the distance. She thought about leaving, about working and living somewhere else. If she moved away, she'd be alone. Far from friends and family. That was the crunch. Was that really what she wanted? She'd always dreamed of having a family of her own and had imagined that was her destiny. But as time marched on, there were fewer and fewer options for a husband in this neck of the woods.

Damnit Maggie! You never used to be this reliant on other people. What had happened to the adventurous Maggie Hayes she used to be? The one who'd backpacked around Europe, waiting on tables to fund the next leg of her journey? As Jace had pointed out, leaving didn't mean forever. Then again, maybe Sturt's Crossing wasn't meant to be her forever home.

The idea struck her how wonderful it would be to travel with a companion.

Someone special – like Jace?

Somewhere special – like Antarctica?

She gave a little cough to cover her confusion. "I love this part of the world. I'd miss it if I left."

"The rich red of the soil is amazing," Jace agreed as he sent the car zooming along at a safe speed over the dirt road.

Maggie stared at the scenery as if at that very instant she would be transported to another time, another place and didn't want to miss anything. "Look at that mob of emus. They've got such beady eyes. I always think they're plotting something nefarious." She laughed as the tallest bird stopped pecking at the spindly yellow grass and glared at the passing car. She was thankful that Jace maintained a steady speed, not going too fast after she'd told him the story of Ronald Burke who'd hit a bulldust hole doing a hundred and twenty, rolled his jeep and been killed instantly.

The sedan ate up the miles as they maintained an easy and surprisingly comfortable silence despite the heavily corrugated road. Curiosity however nibbled away. She longed to learn more about the man by her side. About his past. About his family; who he was and where he came from. But she'd sensed that topic wasn't something he was ready to share. And to be honest, she had more than enough to think about; her parents' return, their expectations, the rest of her life.

The dark red sand was awash with colour. The dusty green foliage and vivid red petals and the coal-black bulbs of Sturt's Desert Peas and the scrubby, grey-white salt bushes. Desert grasses grew in clumps and the gently undulating land was populated with stunted eucalypt trees, feathery mulgas and the desert blood-woods that provided shady groves where mobs of kangaroos either grazed or dozed. The recent rains had caused flowers and plants to bloom that hadn't been seen for well over a decade. High in the sky a hawk wheeled, casting a small moving shadow.

Maggie pressed her finger on the window control and the glass slid silently down. In an instant the cabin was full of the hot thick air of the Outback, and she sucked in a lungful. "Nowhere else in the world could smell like this – it's so rich and always makes me feel alive."

About a gazillion flies zoomed inside and she hurriedly closed the window.

"Smells like home," Jace agreed. "Every time I step off a plane, I can't wait to breathe the Australian air again, but I admit Melbourne is nothing like the Outback."

"Melbourne huh? So that's where you're from originally?" She swatted a couple of flies buzzing about her face.

He huffed out a breath as if trying to blow away the fly that'd settled on his nose. It didn't work. He flicked it off with his fingers. "It's where I'm based when I'm in Australia. I have a small apartment that overlooks the Yarra, not that I spend much time there – I'm usually in Antarctica or filing reports in Canberra for the Australian Antarctica Division. I also do a bit of work now and then on Heard Island and the McDonald Islands maintaining or repairing their communication systems when needed."

"You love it don't you?"

"The work can be challenging in those environments, and I love the isolation and how the landscape seems to go on forever."

"You were right – it sounds exactly like the Outback." Smiling, Maggie indicated the passing landscape.

He grinned. "Must be why I like it out here so much."

"And maybe why you chose to come here for a holiday. You were seeking a familiar backdrop because that's where you feel safe." Lifting her feet, she flexed one foot and then the other to improve circulation. They had been travelling for a few hours and her muscles were becoming stiff.

"There's probably something in that," Jace said slowly as if mulling over her words.

"We all need somewhere that's our safety net, Jace, but I don't think it's healthy if it becomes a barrier to experiencing everything that life has to offer."

"What about you?" His voice held more than a hint of challenge. "Just a few moments ago we had this discussion about you never leaving Sturt's Crossing. There's a big difference between feeling compelled to stay rather than wanting to stay."

She turned to examine his face, noting the flared nostrils and flattened mouth. Her words had hit a nerve. And his had certainly hit hers! She bit back her own annoyance. "I don't regret my choices. I do love the region but I admit there's lots of places I want to visit, especially in Australia. I spent a week snorkelling the

Barrier Reef in my twenties and would love to go back."
She shrugged. "You're right, of course. There's probably a
fear of leaving and being alone that I haven't fully
acknowledged. I didn't realise that until..."

"Until...?" Jace prompted after she failed to finish her
sentence.

Until I met you. Someone who was living his dream.
His work and his life sounded fascinating. So far removed
from anything that Maggie had ever experienced. If she
didn't make an effort to attain her own destiny soon, it
would be too late.

Many years ago, a vicar had visited their tiny town.
The words he'd preached popped into her head – *God
helps those who help themselves.*

Maggie switched her gaze to where a buck kangaroo
stood tall scratching his armpit, his eyes narrow and
steadfast as the car sped past. For the first time since the
phone call with Glen, she wondered what her parents
would do with the store. Whether her father's recent
accident would change their minds about travelling
around Australia. Maybe they were coming back to
Sturt's Crossing to stay. Maybe their days of hitting the
road were behind them. Somehow she didn't think so.
And if that was the case, they would assume that she,
Maggie, would be happy to step into the breach. That she
would do what she'd always done; taken up the slack,
help them out, man the store, be the rock in their lives.
And put her own life on hold. Or maybe they had
assumed she had no dreams beyond Sturt's Crossing?
That she was content.

Silence stretched like a taut rubber band between

them then Jace reached over and squeezed her hand. "What is it? Why are you feeling sad?"

The words erupted from her mouth – really they came from the depths of her soul. "I want a family. A husband. Kids. The whole messy, till death do us part, relationship thing." She felt herself blush. Why oh why had she told *him* of all people? The man whose features had so quickly formed onto the faceless husband of her dreams. A tourist. One who at best would only be around for the next few days.

"I can see you with at least eleven red-headed kids at your feet." He flashed a quick grin.

Smiling and relieved he'd chosen to lighten the heavy moment, she whacked his arm. "Not a football team! I was thinking three at the most."

"And living in Sturt's Crossing?"

"Maybe. I'd love a kind of duo life. Six months some-where else then six months at home."

"If you have kids, you'll need access to schools, hospitals."

"I *can* read you know," she said drily.

He laughed. "You know what I mean."

"Yeah, I do." A vision floated in front of her eyes; a little red-haired daughter and two little boys with dark hair. If Jace could read her thoughts right now, he'd probably leap out of the car and run. And never look back! Because from the little she'd learned about him, he wasn't the family man type. She slumped into her seat and fixed her blurry gaze on the road.

He checked the odometer. "How much further?"

Changing the tricky subject. She didn't blame him.

The conversation had become way too personal for people who had only known each other for a couple of days. "There's a turn off coming up in about another ten minutes."

"Is it tarred?" He sounded hopeful.

"Sorry, more gravel and dirt but given we've been driving since dawn, we're not that far."

Soon Blackbird Tor rose above the landscape, a reddish orange outcrop of granite and ironstone with ridged sides and a flat top. Scrubby bushes clung for footholds on its sides along with some twisted, dwarfed trees.

"That's quite an impressive sight." Jace thumbed toward the windscreen as he leaned forward as if trying to get a better look.

"Around here, we call the tors 'jump-ups'."

"Good to know. Who owns the land surrounding the tors?"

"Blackbird Tor and several surrounding acres was originally part of Flat Rock Station but after the death of Luke's grandfather, it was split up between his dad and his Aunt Claire. When his aunt passed away, it was discovered she'd willed her portion to Rosie who was her goddaughter. Recently and after discussions with the local Elders, Rosie had the title deed changed to incorporate the local First Nations community. They share equal responsibilities in managing the land, the Tor and everything that goes with it. That includes the tourist venture."

"Really?" He shot her an incredulous glance.

Maggie nodded. "Rosie's a firm believer that the land

we all live on was never properly ceded from the original owners."

"I've never given that aspect much thought." Jace frowned then added, "But I approve of her decision."

"I think it's fabulous what she's done. Luke was totally on board which helped. His father did a fair bit of huffing and puffing when Rosie first mentioned it but eventually came around to her way of thinking." Maggie chuckled as she recalled the bluster Old Man Williams (as he was known around town) had spewed forth.

"I can imagine."

A signpost appeared indicating they were approaching the designated camping area and her thoughts couldn't help jumping back in time to when Rosie and Luke had been ambushed by a desperate neighbour armed with a gun. Goosebumps pebbled over her arms, and she sent up a word of gratitude that her friends had survived the encounter.

Jace slowed the car and turned onto a narrow bumpy road which wound around the scrubby bushland. Eventually the track opened up to a cleared area where bush toilet facilities made from local timber with tin roofs sat at the far end of the clearing. A small commuter bus was parked off to one side and there were six glam tents pitched around a cold fire pit encircled with a pile of stones. A shade gazebo had been erected over a long plastic trestle table and a pile of plastic tubs. Several camping chairs sat outside the tents but there was no one else around – apart from ten camels snoozing in a roped off coral beneath a grove of shady trees. One of the camels heaved to its feet and poked an inquisitive nose over the rope fence.

Jace pulled up beside the bus and killed the engine. "Wonder where everyone is."

"They must be exploring the caves on Blackrock Tor. Or looking for clues." Grinning, Maggie snicked off her seat belt and Sherman gave a massive yawn before sitting up to look out the window. He whined. "OK boy, I know exactly how you feel." Smiling she turned to Jace. "We're going to stretch our legs in the direction of the loos. Won't be long and then I'll help unpack the car."

"It's not a problem. I'll deal with our bags. Any idea which tents may be ours?"

"Hang on a sec." Maggie fished out her mobile from the backpack at her feet and did some scrolling. "Here it is – Mason says our names should be taped to the front of the tents. And he also says that we have to share."

Not a muscle moved on his face as his gaze met hers. "Together?"

She blushed. "No with the other tourists. There's a family from Germany who have a tent to themselves. Then two separate tents for the males and another two for the females. The remaining tent is for the tour guide and driver."

"All good." His calm voice gave no indication whether he was disappointed or relieved over the arrangements.

As for Maggie, she couldn't deny that *she* certainly was downright disappointed. But a whole weekend in the company of an attractive man who drew her like no other couldn't be sneezed at. She'd make the most of their time together and hang the consequences.

Snatching up her pack, she opened the car door. She headed for the bush toilets while Sherman sniffed out the best clump of grass to attend to his own business. It didn't matter they weren't sharing a tent, and that probably was for the best. The buffer of other people around could prove another blessing. She'd enjoy the moment, treat the weekend as a gift and hope like hell those silly daydreams of having Jace in her life permanently would soon wither and die.

And that he'd forget her confession about longing for a family of her own.

She pushed open the loo door, feeling confident she could keep her boundaries sturdy and unbroken. A few minutes later, and she was standing outside one of the tents where Jace had dragged her luggage. Sherman gave an excited woof and trotted over to investigate one of the camels. Maggie rushed over in his wake as the camel lowered his head and sniffed at the little dog. Sherman erupted into a frenzy of shrill barks, loud enough to raise the dead. It certainly roused the other sleeping camels who lurched to their hooves. Two ambled over to the rope and tiny puffs of red dust billowed up.

"Sherman! Heel." Maggie grabbed the end of the lead and crouched down beside the dog. Obeying but panting like made, Sherman sniffed back at the camels. Once they'd made friends, she led the dog back to where Jace waited outside a tent with a water bottle in his hand.

"I'm famished." Jace handed the water to Maggie then indicated where he'd filled a bowl of water for the dog. Sherman rushed to the bowl and slurped like there was no tomorrow.

"Thankyou. Gosh yes, I'm hungry too. I wonder how long before everyone returns?" Shuffling until she stood under the narrow wedge of shade from the tent, Maggie took several mouthfuls of water.

As she spoke a *'Hoi'* came from the track and a pink-faced Mason emerged leading a straggling line of sweating people. At the rear, strolled a middle-aged First Nations man with white stubble over his shaven skull and whose face split into a wide grin when he spotted them revealing several missing teeth.

Maggie waved and called out a hello.

"Finally! I thought you'd never arrive!" Mason bustled over and enveloped her hand in both of his. His brown hair didn't have the fiery tint of his brother Luke's but their broad smiles were almost identical. Leaning forward, he gave her a noisy kiss on the cheek. He wore a powder blue, long sleeved shirt and beige pants that were liberally coated with red dust. His eyes twinkled at her from between the bobbing corks hanging from the wide brim of his hat.

Mason had been in a class a few years below her at school but left the area with his mother after his parents split up. Although, she hadn't known him particularly well growing up, since Rosie's advent into his life that had all changed. Her bestie and Mason had brought fresh hope to a community that had been on its knees. Everyone in town wanted them to succeed with their venture. Unfortunately, like so many others, it had ground to a halt when Covid struck. This was the first tour since they had started the business a few years ago.

"Mason. This is Jace."

"Oooh, how lovely." Mason fluttered his eyelashes at Jace as they shook hands, then gave Maggie a dramatic wink.

"Love the hat," Maggie chuckled.

"Tyler loves it too." Bending down, he petted Sherman and sent the bobbles swinging.

Sherman leaped up, his small jaws snapping thinking the hat was some kind of game.

"Oh no you don't, you naughty dog." Smiling, Mason quickly straightened out of his reach.

"Is he here?" Maggie asked, referring to Mason's partner in both business and life.

"He left me in charge of this lot. Thank heavens I say for Uncle Ed who is like the best guide ever!" Mason rolled his eyes as he adjusted his hat. "Tyler says camels are not his thing. As if they're mine! But someone has to do it. He's up at the house. Bonding with dear old Dad." Beckoning for them to follow, he walked over to where the tourists had slumped into their camp chairs and were either guzzling down more water or fanning their hot faces with their hats. "Come on, sweeties. I'll introduce you and then it's party time."

CHAPTER
ELEVEN

A late lunch of fruit and fresh-made sandwiches was handed out. The tourists were a friendly mob and keen to learn all they could from the *'newcomers'*. Jace wasn't certain but he did wonder now and then whether Maggie was avoiding him. Whenever his eyes sought her (and that was often he had to admit), she was far from his side, chatting with someone or other. She could be feeling uncomfortable at how she'd unloaded herself to him in the car. He'd experienced a swell of pride that she trusted him sufficiently to divulge her secret dream. Pride that was intermixed with a gnawing hollowness that seemed to spread wider and wider. The realisation of exactly how lonely he truly was, unnerved him.

It all came down to family.

To not being alone.

To being loved.

To belonging.

And how isolated he'd made his life.

Listening to how the German family laughed and teased each other in their heavy accents underscored his own barren existence. If he had a wife, children... His gaze settled on Maggie who was smiling at something Mason was telling her. She wasn't the only one who had decisions to make.

They spent the afternoon riding the camels around the base of the Tor and searching for the clue Mason had hidden in the branches of a scrubby tree. Once back at the camp site, they sat in the shade watching Uncle Ed, an Elder and local guide, give a demonstration on finding and eating bush tucker. Then he told them about the ancient legend regarding how the Sturt Desert Pea came to be - when during *'The Dreamtime'* a beautiful maiden was promised to an older warrior however she had fallen in love with a young man from a different tribe. The story was about love, pain and loss, and Uncle Ed concluded by saying how the First Nations People called the plant *'the Flower of Blood'*. Jace found the tale extremely moving.

Afterwards everyone was given a chore to perform for dinner and it wasn't long before Mason was dishing up a spicy kangaroo stew from the big cast-iron pot simmering on the fire. Shadows had lengthened across the land. In the west the sky was a kaleidoscope of differing shades of purple and grey clouds as the sun, a fireball of orange and red, dipped below the horizon. Uncle Ed lit a fire contained within a circle of stones.

"That meal was something else." Jace placed his spoon in his bowl then mopped up the remaining gravy with the last of his damper.

"Totally agree." Beside him, Maggie lifted the brown bottle she'd brought with her to her lips.

Jace frowned. "Are you drinking alcohol?"

"What?" Looking annoyed, Maggie waved the bottle in the air. Voice ice cold, she snapped, "For your information, this happens to be a blend of kombucha that I make myself. It aids digestion." With a sniff, she rose and took a seat beside Uncle Ed.

Feeling as if he'd made a total arse of himself, Jace took his plate and went over to the gazebo and assisted with the cleaning up. He'd had no right to question her and certainly no right to pass any kind of judgement. Glumly he took the dripping plate from the middle-aged German woman and wiped it dry with the dishcloth.

Mason bustled about organising games and a sing-a-long where everyone joined in. In the comradery of the moment, Jace's discomfort vanished; especially when Maggie chose a place beside him and favoured him with a small smile.

He instantly apologised for his behaviour earlier and she told him not to worry. A half-moon rose throwing a pale glow over the laughing faces turned towards Mason and the youngest tourist, an American from Idaho, while they gave an impromptu *'can can'* demonstration.

"My goodness, I'm beat." Mason fanned himself as he swanned over to their sides. People called out *'goodnight '*and *'Gute Nacht'* and staggered off towards their tents. A couple remained sprawled in their camp chairs, chatting and sipping a last hot cuppa. He checked the time on his phone. "Nine-thirty. Gosh what a day. But I think everyone enjoyed themselves. I must remember to ask for positive reviews on our website. See you tomorrow, sweeties." Mason trotted off to have a word with Uncle Ed leaving them alone.

With a touch of wonder Jace realised that several hours had passed and he hadn't once brooded over the past. Pulling his mobile from his pocket, he checked for messages or missed calls. Nothing. But he couldn't help noticing he only had one bar. Maybe his mother had tried to contact him but failed to get through. He knew full well his father wouldn't have even tried.

"Problem?" Maggie laid a hand on his arm and gave a gentle squeeze with her fingertips.

"Sorry." He shoved the phone away. "That was rude of me."

"It's okay." Firelight flickered over her face revealing concern in her lovely eyes. "I get the feeling something is on your mind."

He took a deep breath and placed a hand over hers where it lay on his arm. The urge to allow her into his life was too strong. "Today is the anniversary of my older brother's death. Every year, my mother arranges a memorial. Every year I make an excuse not to attend."

"Which is why you ended up here." She nodded as if everything now made total sense.

"Yeah."

"Tell me about him. I'd like to know." Her voice was low and soothing, and he fastened onto it as if he was lost at sea.

Maybe he was – maybe he'd never reached dry land again since Doug's funeral. His eyes stung as he related his childhood memories; how he'd always looked up to him and how Doug had always been there for him. "I was sixteen and Doug nineteen when he was diagnosed with multiple myeloma."

At her questioning glance, he added, "It's a type of blood cancer and incurable. The next couple of years were a never-ending round of treatment. Doug was in hospital more than he was home. By this time, I was at uni. The docs asked if the family would volunteer for a bone marrow test to see if we were compatible. They wanted to do a transfusion. I put my hand up. And then the kicker."

He paused remembering how his life had been ripped apart for the second time. "Mother confessed that my father wasn't my biological father. She'd had an affair and when she fell pregnant with me, the bloke hightailed it out of her life. So she pretended as if the affair had never happened and passed me off as my father's son."

"Oh my God! What a terrible shock for you," breathed Maggie. Then leaning over, gently pressed a kiss to his cheek.

His eyes burned. "It was." The words came out gruff and hoarse and resonating with pain.

"Let's go for a walk." Rising, she held out her hand.

Fingers linked, they strolled away from the campfire. Sherman lifted his head to eyeball them, yawned but remained curled up beside their chairs.

"What happened afterwards?" She added quickly, "You don't have to continue if you feel uncomfortable."

"No. I want you to know. I want you to know all about me." He drew her to a stop and took hold of her other hand. "My father took it hard. He withdrew from me – completely. It was if he could no longer bear to look at my face. That time is a bit of a blur to be honest. I remember Dad walking out of the house after Mum had told us, and staying away for several days. I remember the despair I felt that I couldn't help Doug. I remember feeling unbelievably angry with both of them; my mother for keeping such a terrible secret all these years; and my father for looking at me with such disgust. He'd always seemed to be the one that held us all together, the rock we needed - that I needed, then suddenly he wasn't there anymore. After Doug died, our parents separated, then divorced. I've hardly spoken to my mother since. And my father not at all."

"How long ago did all this take place?" Her eyes glistened in the moonlight as if they held a sheen of tears.

Jace's lonely heart twisted at the empathy evident in her sweet face. "Seventeen years."

"That's a long time to be estranged from your family, and to be alone," she said slowly.

"Like you, I guess I pushed aside the idea that too much time was passing. I've kept busy, immersing myself in my career. My father wrote me a letter a few months ago. I still haven't read it."

"Looks like we've both got an elephant in our rooms," she said lightly.

She understood. Whatever she thought of his parents' behaviour she kept to herself, only radiating a depth of concern for him that shuddered and shook the walls he'd erected until he sensed them begin to shatter. And it was if whatever had constricted him deep inside dissolved leaving him loose, free. The words – *come with me* – bubbled in his throat. A light sweat dampened his skin and his heart raced. *Bloody hell! What am I thinking?* Before he could make sense of his churning thoughts, Maggie stepped closer. She drew their linked hands up, resting them on his chest. The scent of coconut, peaches and warm woman enriched the air, flooding his senses.

"I like you Jace."

"I like you too." The words came out gruff, hoarse almost. Hell, was that a ring of desperation in his voice?

He saw her smile in the flickering light given off by the dying fire.

"Are you going to kiss me? Or do I have to make all the moves?" Her words were light, teasing, filled with warmth. Her breath wafted across his chin. Then she placed her lips on his and all rational thought vaporised.

She tasted of ginger, citrus and strawberries. Her body moved against his, igniting erotic images and a desperate longing to take her to his bed then and there; but this wasn't the time or the place. He wanted some-where special for their first time. Hell, he'd make it so special she'd never forget him and never want anyone else.

His hands roamed up and down the length of her, imprinting her soft, full curves into his memory for all time as his breathing deepened and the sounds of the Outback night faded. She felt perfect in his arms as if she belonged, as if she had always been a part of him. A part that had been missing and was now found.

Dragging his lips across the line of her jaw, he found the sensitive spot beneath her ear, licking and nibbling his way down her neck. The way her hands caressed him fuelled his passion, making it burn brighter than it had ever burned before.

"I want you so much," he growled against her satin-soft skin.

"Same. But..."

He lifted his head and stared into her face, willing her to sense the strength of his feelings. And maybe even understand the maelstrom of emotion filling his heart and mind. Lord knew, he barely understood himself. "I know. Soon...though...very, very soon."

She was trembling in his arms. Or was he trembling?

She gave a cheeky grin then whispered, "You can't escape. Don't forget, I know where you live."

They drew apart. Hand in hand, they strolled back to the campsite and Jace couldn't remember when he had ever felt so at peace and content.

CHAPTER
TWELVE

It was well after mid-day Monday when an older model land rover smothered in red bulldust jerked to a rattling halt in front of the B&B's front gate. With a smile on her face, Maggie stepped off the porch. Hat on her head, she moved to greet the elderly gent exiting from the vehicle. "Hi, I'm Maggie. You must be our guest, Mr. McKenzie. Welcome to Sturt's Crossing. Can I help you with your luggage?"

"All good, young lady. I can manage." He settled an ancient, battered Akubra onto his sparse white hair and creaked open the tailgate.

Despite his protestation, Maggie hurried over. The old codger looked so thin that the slightest of breezes would blow him over. The last thing she needed was a compensation claim on her doorstep. "Please. Allow me to help – it's all part of the service." She flashed him a big smile.

Mr. McKenzie gave a grudging nod. "Very well." He

shuffled out of the way so Maggie could reach in and grab the holdall.

"Is this all you have?"

He jabbed a thumb over his shoulder. "Got one of those bags with wheels on the back seat."

"No worries. I'll see to it." Holdall in one hand, she soon had the rest of his luggage out of the 4WD. "There's a carport out the back. I can move your car for you while you have a bite to eat. I know its past lunch time, but I've a salmon salad in the fridge ready to serve you in the dining room, and there's some leftover brownie slices that I made the other day. Would you also like a hot cuppa?"

"Sounds just the ticket." The elderly bloke cracked a sudden smile that chased away the heavy lines carved into his forehead. Given his weathered skin he had the appearance of a man who'd spent a lifetime under the harsh Australian sun.

Maggie snuck another glance as she herded him up the path and into the house. His clothes were good quality if faded; a pair of beige moleskin pants was teamed with a buttoned white and khaki check long sleeve cotton shirt. He wore slightly scuffed but well-cared for hiking boots on his feet. After he signed in, she showed him around the house then placed his luggage into his bedroom. Leaving him to get settled she went to the kitchen and put the kettle on. Once the tea was brewed, she brought the bone china tea pot over to where her new guest sat at the heavy mahogany table then left returning a moment later with the cold salad dish.

Jace was there and helping himself to a brownie slice. He looked up, a smile lighting his face. She hadn't seen him since breakfast and couldn't deny how the very sight of him sent a quiver through her heart strings.

They'd obviously introduced themselves in her absence. She took care not to stare too much at Jace, the hours they'd enjoyed together over the past weekend still bright and shiny. It wouldn't do to reveal exactly how much those two days had meant to her. How awed and humbled she'd felt when he'd shared his past pain. How desperately she'd wanted to give him comfort. They'd arrived back late at night and spent a lovely couple of hours holding hands as they sat quietly on the veranda and watched the stars.

And then there were those kisses they'd shared that still had her lips tingling. Who could forget that? Or the way her body had fired to life. Everything seemed new. As if she was seeing and experiencing the world for the first time.

There had been that one tense moment when she'd waited, yearning, for him to ask to share her bed. But it had passed and she still wasn't certain whether she was relieved or sad.

Her heart pounded, her knees turning liquid as a sudden shyness hit her. With a clatter she laid the tray on the table hoping for a quick getaway to hide the flood of emotion.

"Join us," the old man said in a manner that indicated he was used to giving orders and having them carried out in an instant.

Jace rose to his feet and pulled out a spare chair

for her.

Face hot as hades, Maggie poured out the tea and pushed the milk and sugar bowls closer. She eyed the two men over the brim of her cup as she sipped, and the men began to eat. They were discussing the politics of the day and giving their opinions on the latest news coming out of Canberra, always a favourite pastime of any Aussie. The old man was picking at his salad as he held his own in the impromptu debate revealing his mind was still sharp and he was someone who kept up to date with the latest news of the world.

What with his expensive clothes but rackety old car, he presented a bit of a conundrum. Maggie wondered what he did for a living – or what he used to do because surely he had to be well into his late eighties? Maybe even older. She'd taken a peek at the register but like Jace, he hadn't completed the address section.

What was it with people these days? A paranoia spurred by the growing social media frenzy where every tiny aspect of a person's life was shared for the world to comment on and see?

When there was a lull in the conversation, she asked, "What brings you to Sturt's Crossing, Mr. McKenzie?"

Leaning back, he wiped his mouth with the linen napkin even though he'd eaten very little of what was on his plate. "That was lovely, Maggie. Thank you. You were asking why I'm here – I guess you could call it a kind of pilgrimage. I wonder if you wouldn't mind showing me the cemetery a little later on? I'd like a lie down for an hour or so first, though."

"Of course. I'd be delighted." Maggie stood and

began to clear up. As soon as she'd done the dishes, she'd nip over and open the shop for a while then close it back up after her guest had rested.

"I wouldn't mind tagging along." Jace gave an easy smile. "Old cemeteries can be fascinating."

"That's settled then." Mr. McKenzie pushed to his feet, gave a minute wobble before ambling off to his bedroom.

"Like a hand with the dishes?" Jace placed his empty cup on the saucer.

"All good. I'll use the dishwasher. I'll be at the store for a while. If you could send me a text when Mr. McKenzie is ready that would be appreciated."

"No worries." He disappeared down the hall and a moment later, she caught the murmur of his voice as he spoke with Sherman. There was the patter of nails on the wooden floor and Jace's soft tread. Then silence.

She wondered if he'd read his father's letter yet. Then wondered whether she dared ask. It would be wiser not to learn too much more about him. She really should keep her distance from a man who was here one day but would be gone the next. But that was so hard when he occupied her every waking thought.

Maggie gathered a pile of plates and glasses and after rinsing them in a large plastic dish half-filled with water, placed them in the dishwasher. She popped the left-over food into Tupperware containers worrying that the old man had eaten very little. Maybe she should have offered something different. A steak with chips. Or perhaps the heat of the day had evaporated his appetite. She made a mental note to question him again about any dietary requirements and his food preference.

Her phone sang that she had received a text as she closed the cupboard door and her nerves tightened when the caller ID flashed on the screen. Glen. After checking to make sure the two men weren't waiting for her outside in the heat, she read the text.

'MUM AND DAD ON THURSDAY MAIL PLANE. SHLD BE HOME LATE FRI. CATCH YOU SIS.'

Typical of Glen telling her almost nothing! Maggie tapped in a message to her mother. Waited. And as usual, there was no response. It did nothing to ease her concern. How severe were her father's injuries? How much should she worry? Or maybe they were minimal and her parents were simply flying home for a fleeting visit. Leaning against the wall, she pinched the bridge of her nose before straightening and meeting Jace's concerned gaze. He stood in the doorway, Sherman panting at his feet, no doubt alerted by the noise of her phone going off. She relayed the latest news then pinned a bright smile on her face as she snatched her hat and left the house. She had a store to mind.

Behind the church, sprawled a haphazard pile of crumbling gravestones set amongst straggly Mitchell grass that made up the local cemetery. The church itself was built from sandstone bricks sometime in the 1880's. These days it was used only for weddings and funerals, and a monthly service by a priest from Walgett. A couple of gum trees and three stunted mulga trees dotted the area providing scattered shade from the searing sun with their thin foliage. Not a breath of a breeze rustled the dry leaves.

"I can't believe how hot it is for November." Jace blew out a gusty breath as he marched along, on the other side of Mr. McKenzie.

Sherman had declined the lure of a walk, preferring his bed beneath the air conditioner. Wise move on his part.

Maggie peered around the old man's thin form to meet Jace's gaze. "This is nothing. Wait until after the New Year when it's the middle of summer. We can reach temps of forty-nine degrees."

She giggled at his horrified expression.

Flinging his arms out, Mr. McKenzie suddenly veered sideways, as his ankle turned when he stepped on a large rock. "Arh!"

Quickly, Maggie grabbed one arm to steady him, noting that Jace had done the exact same thing.

Over the old man's head their gazes met.

She was pleased to note there was no trace of irritation on Jace's face. Her chest swelled. She couldn't stand people who had no patience with the elderly or infirm.

Jace quirked his eyebrows, and her cheeks heated as she realised she'd been gaping at him for several seconds.

Again.

Damn his chiselled jaw.

"No need to cling onto me you two. I'm not an invalid." Mr. McKenzie shook off their hands like an irritated dog. He stopped walking and yanked his faded hat further down his forehead so only the lower half of his face was visible. His large bulbus nose quivered as he snorted in a noisy breath. "Now then. Give me a minute. I need to remember exactly..." his voice trailed off as he frowned at the desolate looking ground. Weeds, stickybeeks, and burrs were a testament to the aridness of the landscape. No flowers brightened the bleak scene.

"It's a disgrace. Doesn't anyone look after this place?" He shot a glare in Maggie's direction.

She shrugged even as she squirmed a little under his accusing eyes. "We have a working bee once a year to clean it up as best we can. That's in May. But it's hard yakker as a lot of the graves are very old. The past few years, we always seemed to be on water restrictions."

"I suppose that's something." Grumbling under his breath, he stomped off, this time moving faster than before. His back had straightened as if now his goal was close, he'd received a burst of energy.

With a wary eye on the uneven ground, Maggie kept pace.

"I remember now. I buried her under that tree." McKenzie's wavering finger pointed at a mulga tree that grew a few metres away.

Maggie pitched forward and would have fallen on her face if Jace hadn't caught hold of her. Her belly fluttered even as her heart thudded hard.

"Easy goes it." His hands tightened over her waist, and she found herself cuddled against his hard, warm body. He lowered his voice to whisper near her ear, "Did you hear what he just said? Or did I dream it?"

Their gazes shot to the old man heading toward the tree with purposeful strides.

"I don't..." Maggie croaked. She shifted in Jace's embrace to stare into his widened eyes. His expression told her he was just as startled. All those thriller movies and lurid crime novels she read screamed to life in her mind. "*He said he buried her.* What if...Of heavens! What if I've let a murderer into my home? What if he's wanted by the police!" Her voice rose to a shriek.

The old man stopped and turned around to stare at them with narrowed eyes.

Maggie gave a little finger wave and forced her lips into a smile.

"Shush!" Jace's jaw worked. "What do you know about him?"

"Only the info he put in the register which was stuff all." Lowering her voice, Maggie gave him a hard stare as she pulled away. "Actually, I know as much about him as I do about you."

Jace snorted. "But I'm not a killer."

"I don't even know if Jones is your real name."

"Does it matter?"

She chewed her lip, feeling troubled. "Yes, it does. It's a matter of trust."

His eyes fastened on her mouth and her heart tripped over. "It's De Haven. See? I trust you." Raising his head, his intense gaze met hers.

Desire hot and hungry stirred beneath her breast and she swayed closer until a mere breath stood between their bodies.

"What are you two doing over there?" hollered Mr. McKenzie.

Flustered, she pulled away.

His hands slipped slowly down her arms as he whispered, "Later."

Later? She was in too deep already. The smart thing to do, would be to set firm boundaries and stay well behind them. She had a sinking feeling her heart was yelling *'the smart thing to do could go to hell'*. Damn his deep, dark eyes.

Struggling to ignore the race of her pulse and the fluttering in her belly, she muttered over her shoulder, "The old guy is who we've got to check out later, not fool around."

Then charged off to where Mr. McKenzie had stopped beside the tree. After giving her a searching look, the old bloke lowered his head. A deep sigh rattled from his bony chest. Maggie made sure there was more than an arm's length between them in case he made a move to attack her. Frowning, she eyed his frail physique. Not that he could be much of a threat since he looked as if a puff of air would send him toppling to the ground. He had to have been joking. Or maybe he was delusional or suffered from dementia. He'd been nothing but polite if a little crusty at times since the moment he'd stepped into the B&B.

Just because he has good manners means nothing, Maggie. Remember Ted Bundy!

Heavens above, she didn't know what to think.

With a loud crack of his knees, Mr. McKenzie crouched to yank a weed out of the ground, then tossed it aside. "I knew it was wrong at the time. But what could I do? My Beth loved that little dog so much I had to put her as close to her grave as possible."

"Oh my...you're talking about a pet?" squeaked Maggie.

Straightening, Mr. McKenzie's bushy brows twitched. "What the devil do you think I'm talking about?"

With a face so hot she could have fried eggs on her cheeks, Maggie didn't dare look at Jace who'd burst into a fit of coughing. No doubt to mask his hoot of laughter. She muttered, "I got a little confused."

And I'm not the only one! Hiding her relief and the urge to giggle, she cleared her throat. "I didn't realise you had relatives in town, Mr. McKenzie."

"Of course, I do. Wouldn't have come to this godforsaken place otherwise." He snorted. The fire left his voice as he mumbled, "Well, what I mean is only Beth that I know of, and she's long gone. This is where we met." A tear creased down his leathery cheek.

He sounded so lonely Maggie felt her heart clench in empathy. Whatever was his family thinking? Allowing such a frail old man wander about the Outback alone. Unless there was no one else. "Here in Sturt's Crossing?"

"Yep. But that was almost a lifetime ago. Tiffany was her toy poodle. They were devoted to each other and after Beth passed, the poor thing seemed to simply fade away. I made sure they were together again. I'm talking years ago, of course. That's Beth's resting place, the one with the granite gravestone and the pink marble plaque.

The vacant lot beside her, is reserved for me." He swayed a little as he pointed to the grave closest to the tree.

Jace took hold of his elbow and led him over to a nearby tomb. "Let's sit down for a while, shall we?"

Another tear wormed its way down the lined cheek as the old man slumped forward, hands clasped together. "She wouldn't be proud of what I've done. I messed things up good and proper."

"I'm sure that isn't true," murmured Maggie.

"What would you know?" His eyes were hard and cold as he shot her an irritated glare. His shoulders slumped as he seemed to deflate suddenly. "I'll soon join her. But I've got a hell of a lot of problems to fix first." He rambled on.

Maggie couldn't make out the rest of his mumbled words even though she leaned as close as she dared.

After a few minutes, Mr. McKenzie fell silent and they all sat there while the sun seared from the sky and sweat trickled down Maggie's back and made her scalp itch. It was hard to know what to say with the old man lost in memories. And judging by his grim expression they weren't pleasant.

Thankfully, Jace eventually broke the awkward silence. "How about we head to the pub and have a cold drink. I don't know about you, but I could do with something to eat." He offered a hand to help the old bloke to his feet, then gently steered him away from the graveyard.

"I'd love to learn more about how you met Beth, Mr. McKenzie," said Maggie as they walked towards the pub.

"Why, you never know. We might be related. My folks have been here since about the dawn of time."

The elderly gent suddenly let out a cackle of laughter. "I doubt it, young lady. Which is just as well because I've got plans for you. I'm going to find you a husband. I've got four sons you know and one of them is bound to tickle your fancy."

Maggie didn't need or want anyone of his four sons. She'd already found the man who *'tickled her fancy'* and filled her dreams. A man soon to leave town and never return.

THIRTEEN

S prawled in one of the white Hampton-style deck chairs that sat on the front porch, Jace sipped his iced tea and smiled. Was that a hint of peppermint he'd tasted? He'd noted the well-kept vegetable and herb gardens in the raised beds the day he'd moved into the B&B, approving of the shade cloth covering and the reticulated water drip system in place. He suspected this was Maggie's handiwork. It seemed she was a woman of many talents. Each hour spent in her company he learned something new about her, and damn if each hour he didn't like her that little bit more.

If he wanted to be honest with himself, like was too tepid a word to explore the myriad of emotions Maggie induced in him. His shoulder-blades twitched as he considered that point then he flattened his mouth. He reminded himself of his vow to avoid complications in his life. That relationships for him were not meant to be. Like what had happened with his parents? Both had failed him when he'd needed them most although it was his father's defection which had hurt the most.

He knew in his gut Maggie wasn't the kind of girl who'd be into a brief fling. No, she was the white picket fence type of girl, probably with a small mob of kids at her feet. A small-town girl who deserved better – and he'd better bloody well not forget it, or they could both end up hurt.

He hadn't missed the warmth in her eyes each time she looked at him. It would be too easy to yield to the temptation to kiss her pink lips again. That way lay madness. Because the problem was, more than attraction sizzled between them.

And *he* had his future all mapped out in front of him. After his mother's revelation that had destroyed his world, he'd made plans that didn't include any kind of family whatsoever.

Jace took a long swallow of his drink and stared glumly out into the darkness. Now, who was he kidding? Those plans made so long ago no longer held appeal. It was about time he admitted he didn't want to spend the rest of his life alone. And there was the other problem – Maggie herself. Her family would arrive this week. A lurch in his gut told him how anxious he was for her. Had she thought about her life? Decided she wanted more than what this tiny, almost forgotten, town could offer? And what would she do if her parents pressed her to stay? Her father could have a long road ahead of him recovery wise. Maggie, being the loving, caring person that she was, would probably want to help as much as possible.

That would mean – she would stay.

He would leave.

And their paths would never cross again.

From one of the neighbouring houses, a tom cat began to yowl, quickly joined by a chorus line of other cats. Yapping shrilly, Sherman came bolting around the side of the house, skidded across the front yard sending puffs of dust rolling into the air then darted under the bushes. Leaves crackled, twigs snapped, cats squealed and hissed. Sherman barked.

Then all was quiet once more.

Sherman trotted out from under a rosemary bush, tail wagging, panting around a large smirk. Jumping onto the veranda, he collapsed onto the boards with a satisfied sigh.

"Told those cats off, huh boy?" Jace stretched down and gave the little dog a big scratch around his ears.

From the inside of the house, came the clatter of crockery. Taking a deep breath, he drew in the succulent scent of the Moroccan lamb casserole that was on the menu for tonight's meal. His stomach gave a loud rumble.

Head lolling on his chest, Brian McKenzie snorted as he dozed in the chair on the other side of the low coffee table. Then he jerked himself awake, blinking and looking around as if for a few seconds he didn't recognise his surroundings.

Leaning forward, Jace was about to say something reassuring when the old guy straightened.

"Damn fool dream." Brows bunched together in a

scowl he shook his head like he was trying to rid himself of dark thoughts.

Jace remained a respectful silence. He knew all about dark thoughts.

Bitter regrets and haunting memories.

A bloke as old as Mr. McKenzie no doubt had more than his fair share to mourn over.

Jace made a business over pouring iced tea into another glass, the ice cubes chinking together. "Care for a cold drink?"

"Wouldn't say no to that, boy." Brian McKenzie smacked his lips together as he took the glass. "Cheers." He slugged down several swallows before wiping his mouth with the back of his hand. "Where's that girl of ours?"

Heat crawled up Jace's cheeks as he met the old guy's sharp eyes and decided it wasn't worth getting into a debate about *'our girl'*. "Seeing to dinner which shouldn't be too long."

"Good. I'm starving."

Jace smiled politely, while thinking about the other man's poor appetite.

At each mealtime, Brian would say how hungry he was and yet he ate very little, spending a lot of time pushing the food around his plate. But for all that, he was always appreciative and complimented Maggie on her culinary skills. It made Jace wonder whether the old guy was seriously ill.

Giving a sudden grin which revealed surprisingly expensive-looking dentures, Brian pulled out a notebook from his pants pocket and flourished it over the table.

"Check this out. I've made a list of all the suitable blokes in Sturt's Crossing."

"Hmmm," Jace said vaguely. *Suitable for what?*

"Now, don't tell me you've forgotten." Brian shifted in his chair, sending it knocking against the table. The jug containing the last of the iced tea wobbled then settled before it tipped over. "I had a good chat this arvo with Charlie and Larry in the pub going over the candidates."

What is he talking about?

When Jace failed to immediately respond, the old bloke grinned again, looking a bit like a crafty crocodile. "We're working on a husband for Maggie."

Jace's mouth sagged. Snapping it shut, he muttered through his teeth, "We? There is no *'we'*. This was your crazy idea."

"Where's your balls, boy? Come on. You can't deny, Maggie's a fine-looking woman. Or are you blind?"

Jace swore he felt the blood leave his face at Brian's knowing expression. He croaked, "Of course, I noticed."

As Brian slapped the notebook onto the table making it rock again, he snorted. (The old fellow seemed quite fond of snorting when he was irritated – which was often.) "Can't leave here without making sure she's looked after. You and I, we've got responsibilities."

Strewth! The old bloke had only met Maggie that day! Rolling his eyes, Jace wished himself a million miles away from this conversation. "Be serious. This isn't any of our business. It's not your responsibility and it's certainly has nothing to do with me who Maggie marries."

"You're saying it wouldn't bother you to see her joined at the hip with some no-gooder? A drinker or wife beater? Or have her wither away into a lonely, dried-up old woman? Think of what she'd miss out on. A family – kids, a good man who'd be kind to her in the day and know how to bed her in the night."

A family, kids – the kind of life Jace refused to dream was in his own future. His gut twisted. He would definitely *not* think about bedding her in the night!

"For....heaven's sake." Jace's voice came out sounding strangled. He shot a pitiful glance toward the door, wondering if he could make a run for it. But the wily old bloke would probably shuffle after him. The thought of Brian continuing this madness within Maggie's earshot turned his bowels to water. At his feet, Sherman yawned and shifted position. "We need to leave this alone."

Brian flipped open the notebook and squinted at the page. Scowling, he held it closer then moved it further away from his face. "Nope. We're going to see this through – you and I – together."

"Count me out. I am *not* going to get involved."

"Hey? What are you? A man or a mouse?" Brian stabbed the book with a knobbly finger. "We need to get this sorted. And soon. I don't have much time left."

Taking a steadying breath, Jace counted to five before saying, "I wondered whether you might be unwell."

Brian snorted. Again. "No idea what you're talking about. I'm as fit as I can be considering my age. No, I only meant before I leave town. And I guess it won't be long and you'll be on your way too," he said gruffly.

But Jace noted how the old man shifted his gaze to

his right. Should he call him out? Maybe it would be better not to question him more about the subject. If Brian was seriously unwell, he'd hardly want to share with a virtual stranger. "I still have a few days leave left," he said, although in reality he had made no firm commitments to moving on. He'd had some hazy ideas that he might hang around for a while, meet Maggie's family, wait and see if she came to a decision about her life. He clamped his mind shut on any further thoughts only admitting to himself that his reluctance to leave Sturt's Crossing grew stronger with every passing day.

"Then let's get down to it." Brian handed the note-book over.

After reading the – admittedly very short – list, Jace placed the book onto the table. "Okay. So you have ten guys here. Some names I recognise from fellas I met down at the pub but the others - I suppose I could ask the people in town if they know them. But what about these four blokes that don't have a surname written down?"

Looking smug, Brian folded his arms over his bony chest. "You don't need to do any digging about them, boy. They're my sons. And I'm telling you now – you've got some stiff competition there."

Wanting to gnash his teeth, he was saved by a gong clanging from the kitchen. A second later, Maggie's voice floated out the screen door. "Dinner's ready."

Tail wagging like a washing machine, Sherman raced to the door to peer through the screen.

Jace bolted to his feet and stuffed the book back into

the old guy's hands. "You're mistaken. I couldn't care less who Maggie marries."

"Hah! I did wonder." Brian whipped out a pen and wrote down another name.

Unable to resist his curiosity, Jace peered over the other man's shoulder only to see his own name in bold black strokes. Leaving Brian cackling like a proud rooster on the veranda, Jace stalked inside the house, his head whirling with a fantasy he hardly dared hope could come true.

FOURTEEN

T he past three days had flown past. Mr. McKenzie had kept both Maggie and Jace on their toes; what with driving him out to fossick for opals at Blackbird Tor on Tuesday. Wednesday was the long drive to Old Man Williams' sheep station where the two men had disappeared off to the sheering sheds for hours on end. Then later that afternoon, Maggie's guest had insisted on doing a meet and greet of just about every person in town. Exactly what he was up to, she had no idea but she was positive the old fellow had an agenda. He kept scribbling away in his little notebook and often had mumbled conversations with himself.

What with dusting and cleaning her parents' place, then opening and closing the store at odd hours depending on Mr. McKenzie's schedule, she had had very little time to herself. And very little time to think. Exhausted after the long days, she'd quickly fallen asleep each night only to dream of a certain someone who twisted her insides and filled her with a restless yearning.

At least, she'd had the gift of Jace's company every day. Not once had he complained or made excuses to avoid the elderly man. Rather he acted eager to be in her company. Or had she imagined that? What if it was simple good manners keeping him by her side?

After she and Jace had cleaned up following dinner, they'd made their way to the veranda with a jug of iced tea. A faint yellow light spilled from the living room window bathing the area in a soft romantic hue.

Maggie leaned back in the deck chair and tilted her head to the stars. "My parents will be home tomorrow," she said in a low voice, careful not to wake the old man who had sought his bed a few minutes earlier. She frowned as she stared at the Southern Cross. There had been no time for any tete-a-tete's with Jace. His promise in the churchyard of *'later'* had never manifested. Maybe he had had second thoughts.

Pity. She'd been *so* looking forward to *'later'*.

She'd dreamed of nothing else since.

"I imagine you must be looking forward to seeing them again. Have you heard anything more about your father's condition?" Jace sipped his iced tea while Sherman snored on his lap.

"Not a smidgeon." Maggie plucked at a thread hanging from the cushion and sent him a sideways peek. His chiselled jaw was as firm as ever although the line of his lips was relaxed.

Jace shifted, dislodging Sherman who snuffled with irritation at being disturbed and jumped down to curl up beside his feet. "No doubt when your mum arrives, she'll take over running the shop. That'll give you time on your hands to do something for yourself."

He turned to face her, and she noted the sparkling gleam in his eyes. Her pulse ratcheted up several gears and suddenly the cool night air turned hot. He couldn't possibly have read her thoughts – could he? "Like what?" she croaked.

Leaning closer, he slid two fingers down the curve of her cheek. "Like travel. Like exploring different..." he paused a beat. "...options. I've got a few suggestions." His intense stare focussed on her mouth.

Skin heating under the weight of his gaze, she nudged the palm of his hand. "I bet you have." Then her amusement died as confusion and doubt re-surfaced. She suspected she was already in too deep where he was concerned. He was such a determined bachelor she couldn't imagine he had anything more in mind than a brief affair. That wasn't for her. She had to protect what little was left of her heart. "Mum will probably need help with Dad. And there's the store," she mumbled as her spine stiffened.

His hand fell away and he settled back against his chair. "Have you made a decision about what *you* want to do next?"

"If Dad doesn't regain his health, they might sell the RV and stay, especially if he needs on-going medical care." Her shoulders drooped. "Either way, they won't be able to manage by themselves."

"I assume they have friends here who could give them a hand. Or maybe they could hire a nurse."

Tears burned her eyes, and it took three swallows to dislodge the lump in her throat. Her idiotic daydream of exploring the world with Jace crumbled at her feet. She was a fool. "We're not exactly rolling in money."

Jace lowered his head as if he'd found something infinitely fascinating in the dirt. When he didn't respond, she tapped his wrist. But he jerked his hand out of her reach. All the heat and longing she'd felt a few moments ago evaporated.

Finally, he looked at her. No trace of that twinkle in his eyes now. "Don't tell me – you've decided to care for him."

"This is my father we're talking about."

"What about your life? Haven't you wasted enough of it already in this place?" He flung out a hand as if to encompass the entire town of Sturt's Crossing.

"Wasted!" She snapped her gapping mouth shut. "I don't consider living in my hometown, running the family store, being part of a family and community as wasting my life."

He huffed out an irritated breath. His words were curt as if he spoke through clenched teeth. "And that's all you do. Run some ratty shop. Talk to some ancient biddies. And going to the pub is the highlight of your day. Is that what you want for the rest of your life? What about having that family you talked about?"

"You know what? My life is none of your business."

"You're right. It isn't. I just don't like to see people waste what little time we have on this earth hiding from the world." His tone sounded stuffy, all trace of his former anger carefully blanketed.

Maggie jumped to her feet, her hands landing on her hips. "As if you can talk!"

"I've travelled all over the world. I have a job that's exciting and challenging. Better than moping about dreaming of living and doing a stupid vlog no one listens to."

"I'm surrounded by friends, by my family, by people who care about me. From everything you've told me, you travel alone. You're part of a team but I bet you don't interact much with them do you? I bet they don't call to say hi or do fun things with you when they're in town. I bet you haven't phoned your mother back to talk about your brother. I bet you haven't read that letter your father sent, let alone think of calling him even though you said you'd contact him for help with our petition. You say you're living your life. Well, you're not. You're hiding from the world. You have no one to share those experiences with, no one who gives a damn about you." Bending, she plucked a startled Sherman off the floor. "Enjoy your lonely existence, Jace."

Head down so he wouldn't notice the tears falling on her cheeks, Maggie charged into the house, slamming the door behind her.

The next day, Maggie stood beside the rear gate leading into the yard at the back of the shop. She'd spent the morning scrubbing the family's small home from top to bottom. The beds had been stripped and re-made with fresh linen, mattresses had been aired and she'd even washed the windows inside and out. Every room sparkled. She had brightened the dining room with a vase of freshly cut bunch of Sturt Desert Peas. Everything was as perfect as possible.

She should be feeling excited at the thought of seeing her parents again. However, all she felt was a sickening sense of dread. Having a sleepless night where she'd picked over everything she'd said and everything Jace had said hadn't helped. They'd both lashed out –trying to sabotage something so special it had sent them scurrying back to their safe place? Oh how she wished she'd reined in her temper. That bitter argument with Jace just wouldn't leave her thoughts and there was an ache in her heart that wouldn't ease. She pressed a shaking hand to her chest and breathed deeply, willing away the wash of fresh grief that chilled her to her core. Neither of them had referred to the previous night when they'd met over breakfast. They had spoken so politely and so coldly to each other that Mr McKenzie's attention had been caught. He'd kept looking at them and smirking. She was glad he was now ensconced in the B&B safely occupied with Charlie who had dropped by for a chat. He'd seemed more weary than usual, with an odd greyness to his complexion which was concerning.

Sliding her mobile phone out she checked the time. Jace had left fifteen minutes ago. Despite the chilliness between them, he had offered to drive to the emergency air-strip and pick up her parents while she performed any last minute chores. Snake as well as Senior Constable Anderson had also offered but her father needed a comfortable ride and neither of their vehicles would quite fit that bill. And no way could she allow her father be carted into Sturt's Crossing inside a police car. He'd never forgive her.

Tyres crunched over gravel, and she wiped her clammy palms over her shorts. Glen had texted earlier warning her that their father no longer resembled the robust man he'd once been. Her heart thudded hard. Suddenly, she had no idea what to expect.

Jace's car rolled to a halt, and he hopped out to open the rear door.

For a few seconds, Maggie almost failed to recognise the wizened figure leaning out of the car, one leg encased in plaster, one arm in a sling. The last time she'd seen him, he'd sported a full head of thick grey hair. His stance had been upright, his figure stocky with a substantial beer belly. Now his hair was snow white and wispy, and his body thin and stooped. "Dad!" She darted forward and gave him a gentle hug. Eyes wide, her gaze sought her mother now helping Jace to unfold the wheelchair which he'd taken from the car boot.

Her mother bustled over and kissed her cheek as Jace manoeuvred her father out of the car. "You look different, Maggie. Is that makeup you're wearing? Grant, doesn't she look good for a change?"

"What are you talking about Lucy. My girl always looks better than good." Grant Hayes gave Maggie a goofy grin which didn't quite hide the grimace of pain as he settled into the chair.

Her heart turned over. Her dad might be physically diminished by his accident, but he was still the same man who softened her mother's sharp tongue. Smiling, she went to hoist a suitcase from the car while her parents argued behind her.

"I'll deal with the luggage." Jace placed his hands on her shoulders and looked into her face. He drew in a noisy breath, his expression earnest and concerned. "I'm so very sorry, Maggie. I was wrong to say you've wasted your life. I think you're wonderful and an amazing, beautiful woman. You run a business in a difficult environment. You're surrounded by friends and a community who see you as a vital part of their lives. Meeting you has made me realise that I'm the one who has wasted years by shunning my family. I took out my regret with the way I've handled my own life on you. Please say, that you'll forgive me?"

She blinked away the sudden burn in her eyes. "I appreciate your apology. Thank you, Jace. Can we...can we talk about this later?"

"Definitely." A look of intense relief settled on his face and the smile he gave her infused new life into her daydreams.

"Come on, Mum and Dad. I've got the kettle on the boil and fresh scones with cream and jam." She moved towards her parents, feeling an absurd desire to skip with happiness. And hope.

"Excellent. I'm famished. Come on in too, Jace. I want to hear more about Antarctica. After Maggie's filled me in on everything that's been happening here of course," Grant said over his shoulder as Lucy pushed the wheelchair over the rocky ground.

Soon everyone was seated around the battered kitchen table. Her father had insisted on remaining in his wheelchair, saying it was too hard switching back and forth. Sweat beaded his lined face and his free hand trembled as he reached for a scone.

Maggie launched into the scant doings of their town, remembering to relay their suspicion of a mine rep lurking about and finished up with a brief mention of the other guest in Rosie's B&B.

"Sounds like you've been busy." A blob of jam and cream clung to her father's lower lip.

Without saying a word, Lucy calmly stretched over and wiped his mouth with a napkin as if he was little more than a toddler.

"Business good?"

"About the same, Dad." Maggie fiddled with her cup handle, far too aware of the man sitting silently beside her enjoying the simple fare. Jace's hesitant smile, his heartfelt apology whirled inside her mind along with a fragile hope for a different future as she tried to concentrate on her parents. It was obvious it would take a long time before her father was back to his normal self. Was now a good time to ask about their plans? Suddenly, she couldn't bear to wait any longer. "Tell me what happened. I need to know what's needed to aid your recovery."

Her parents exchanged one of those glances long-time married couples communicate with before Lucy said, "You know how your father fell off the RV. I did warn him…"

Grant rolled his eyes. "Don't start, Lucy."

She carried on as if he hadn't spoken. "If he'd listened to me this would never have happened. You know the extent of his injuries and about the operation. He has strict instructions to rest until he has regained some strength. We've been shown a series of exercises for him to perform before his next specialist appointment in three weeks' time." Lucy took a sip of her tea.

"Where's the specialist located, Mum?"

"Newcastle."

"You'll need someone to drive you to the coast and back." Maggie knew her father wasn't fond of her mother driving long distances. They had probably already roped Glen into that duty.

Grant chipped in, shaking his head. "This won't be a quick return trip. Your mother will drive as we'll be gone for some time."

"You're letting Mum drive the RV?" Maggie's voice rose to a squeak.

"Of course not. We'll take your jeep. It's not as if you use it much. Basically, Maggie, I'm doing rehab until the cast comes off, and for some months after that as well. The doc wants me to attend physios, remedial massages, you name it. He's got me booked in for ages. We're just home for the next few weeks because they needed the hospital bed." He patted Maggie's hand and smiled. "And of course, I wanted to see you, pet."

"So you're leaving in three weeks' time? It sounds like you won't be home for Christmas either." Maggie's head throbbed. It sounded as if they had it all planned out. And without asking her once if she minded being without a vehicle for an extended period of time. She didn't dare look in Jace's direction.

"That's correct. Once your father starts his rehabilitation, I don't want to break the momentum." Lucy gave Maggie a sharp glance. "You could always come to us for Christmas. Catch the coach bus to Sydney then train up to Newie. We've organised a rental property for the duration, so we'll have a spare bedroom. The RV can stay here until we've made a firm decision."

Something cold and hard lodged in the pit of Maggie's belly. She had a feeling she wasn't going to like what came next.

Grant cleared his throat. "You see, pet. With you running the store, we reckon we can afford it. We're considering moving to the coast, permanently."

FIFTEEN

After the bombshell Maggie's parents had dropped, her father had retired to a bedroom to rest while her mother had unpacked their cases. Jace had assisted Maggie with clearing away the table then walked with her to the store. Her silence worried him. It was hard to gauge what she was thinking or feeling from the closed expression on her face. But the paleness of her features screamed its own tale. He wanted to shout and yell at the Hayes saying, *'Can't you see you're killing your only daughter's options?'* Of course, Maggie could well be perfectly content moulding her life to suit their expectations. She may have decided to stay where she was needed; where she had made her home. But for Maggie's sake, he hoped not. She deserved a chance to live her dreams.

He retreated to the cottage where Mr. McKenzie took one look at his face and disappeared into his bedroom. He returned a moment later bearing a bottle of whiskey.

"I could do with a little nip myself," he said, pouring

out generous measures into a couple of glasses. "Here's to the people we loved. And lost." Brian drained his glass in one gulp.

"Thanks." Jace took an appreciative sip, enjoying the warmth of the alcohol slipping down his throat.

"You know what they say – a problem shared..." The old man waggled his bushy eyebrows at Jace.

Then somehow it all came spilling out; his estrangement from his family tangled up in concern over Maggie and his growing feelings for her. Feeling drained, he slumped in the chair and moodily regarded the whiskey in his hand, thinking about last night and how he'd been about to ask her to come with him and how he'd hesitated as doubt had struck. He'd wondered whether she needed to make that important decision to leave all by herself. Besides, she wanted a family when the very thought of family usually caused a cold sweat to break out all over him. Funny how that particular dread had dissipated these past days. When Maggie had stated how she intended to hang around and help her parents, a tide of frustration, hurt and disappointment had swamped his control. Instead, he'd said something absolutely hateful about wasting her life. What a pissant he was. Because she had been correct. He was the one hiding from facing the past and his parents. Well, all that was about to change. The sight of what had been a healthy middle-aged man shrunken by pain had shaken him. That could be his own father. For all Jace knew, his father might no longer enjoy good health. He had to reach out before it was too late regardless of what had happened in the past.

"Don't see there's much to think about, son. You either want Maggie in your life or you don't. Same with your family. Make the decisions, then move forward."

Jace met the older man's rheumy eyes. "I think I already have - I just haven't admitted it."

"No point in waiting for some kind of sign from heaven to tell you it's the right choice. Take it from me; that isn't going to happen. No one knows what life has in store. We simply make the best decision at the time and do our best to make sure everything works out." Brian McKenzie tossed back the last mouthful of whiskey and wiped his mouth with the back of one wrinkled hand.

"What about yourself? I reckon you've also got some decisions to make."

The old man shifted his gaze to stare into the middle distance. "Already done, son." He shook his head slowly, his expression turning into something close to grim acceptance. "I won't be here though to see if it all turns out the way I hope."

Jace murmured, "I'm sorry, mate. Anything I can do?"

"Not really, but thanks all the same. I've got my solicitor arriving in a few days to tidy up the last lot of loose ends. Don't worry. I don't intend to kick the bucket where Maggie will be the one to find me. Got myself booked into a nursing home in Walgett. I move in next Wednesday." The old man shrugged before giving a quick crafty grin and saying, "If you don't get cracking son, I'll put Maggie back on my *'to fix before I cark it'* list." Placing both hands on the armrests of his cane chair, he heaved to his feet and picked up his half-empty whiskey bottle. "Think I'll have a lie down."

Smiling his appreciation, Jace considered the last mouthful in his glass before pushing the drink to one side. He looked up when he heard the soft tread of footsteps coming his way then rose to greet one of Maggie's neighbours.

Jace took yet another steaming casserole from the woman looking up at him from the bottom of the steps.

The South African lady murmured, "Please let Maggie know, we are here if she needs us. Mosa Botha is my name. My husband and I run the petrol station."

"I'll pass on your message. Thank you." He gave another friendly smile when the woman waved to him before trotting down the path. She wasn't the first to offer help. Since lunch time, people had been knocking on the B&B with food or notes of support. Not wanting to disturb the Hayes after their long journey, they had fronted Jace asking him to pass on their good wishes.

The bushes rustled and Sherman sidled out to sit at his feet, tail wagging, tongue hanging out. Jace sat the Pyrex dish onto the rustic table then found a dish and filled it with fresh water for the dog.

Jace took an appreciative sniff of the casserole's contents, before taking it into the kitchen. When he returned with a small raw bone for Sherman, he found Maggie leaning on the railing and staring out into the hot afternoon sun.

"Something smells good," she said in a low voice.

"I'm fairly sure its Cape Malay curry with saffron rice."

"Mrs. Botha has been here? She's a fantastic cook. That was very kind of her."

Jace handed the bone to Sherman who all but snatched it from his hand and scampered under one of the chairs to begin gnawing. "You've got enough food now to feed an army."

Maggie turned around, and he had to school his face not to wince at the sight of the shock still evident in her wide eyes. "I appreciate your help today."

Hunching his shoulders, he strolled over and placed his hands palm down on the railing. "Not a problem."

They stood a few moments in silence while the heat caused Jace's shirt to stick to his back. He dithered for a moment wondering whether he should pop his hand under her elbow and urge her to sit then decided that she may not thank him for treating her like broken glass. Maggie was tougher than she looked, with her mane of red curls and pale skin. Her chin was firm and her shoulders straight and he couldn't help a warm glow of pride in her resilience. She was a true woman of the outback – able to weather any storm. She would be an awesome wife – and mother. But he longed to show he was there for her.

And then that magic moment.

Her fingers touched his.

Without glancing in her direction, he linked his hand with hers enjoying the electric frizz from her touch. It was more than passion; more than desire; maybe something better and stronger that would stand the test of time – friendship and true love. "How's your father?"

"Resting. Mum took a lie down as well and since there was no one about, I shut the shop for an hour." She sighed and turned to face him. "I admit it was quite a shock seeing him again. I wasn't prepared for how much the accident has affected Dad's physical appearance."

"I remember when Doug underwent his first treatment, and I visited him in hospital. I almost didn't recognise him."

"Have you heard from any of your family?"

He shook his head. "My mother hasn't phoned since the day I arrived when I told her I wouldn't be at the service."

"Nothing from your father then?"

"No."

"Have you read his letter yet?"

Jace met her gaze and touched the top pocket of his shirt, hearing the faint crackle of paper. "I was thinking of doing just that this afternoon."

Maggie went to slip her hand from his, but he tightened his grip. She raised her eyebrows. "Want some privacy?"

"Not really. I'd like you to stay – only if you wish though. You have your own problems."

Somehow she seemed to be standing taller. The shock had faded from her eyes, replaced with deep compassion and he found himself longing to kiss her again. She tilted her head, saying, "First, your letter."

Drawing in a deep breath, Jace unfolded the two sheets and began to read. After a few seconds, he met Maggie's steady gaze. "I can't...I don't..." Eyes stinging he swallowed, as memories flooded his mind and hope swelled full and hard in his chest. After several long seconds, he managed to croak out the words he hardly dared believe were written on the paper he held in shaking fingers, "He apologises for punishing me by pushing me away. That he knows what happened had nothing to do with me. Says he wants the opportunity to reconcile and beg my forgiveness if I'll give him the chance."

Eyes shining, Maggie placed a hand on his arm and gave a gentle squeeze. Somehow her presence steadied him and he carefully folded the letter, placing it back in his pocket. "That sounds positive. What are your thoughts, though?" Maggie asked.

"I'd already made my decision, but his letter clinches it. I'm leaving for Melbourne. I'll visit my father and take it from there." He gave a wry grimace. "I'm even going to beard the dragon - my mother that is and meet up with her. Take it slow and see if I can re-connect with both of them."

"I'm happy for you." Maggie smiled and he noticed how she suddenly blinked rapidly as if chasing away tears. Then her chin lifted. "I'll miss you, Jace. But I believe you're doing the right thing for yourself. Whatever happens, you'll know that you've done everything possible to re-kindle your relationship with your parents."

"You've made me realise the value of family and community, Maggie. Of being part of something important." He tugged her close then pulled her gently into his arms. Staring into those brilliant green eyes of hers, he knew he'd found his home.

"I don't know what you've decided to do – but I'm going to throw another suggestion into the mix." His heart all but leapt from his chest, so fierce were his heartbeats. Time for him to take a chance on a different future. "Come with me and share my life. I don't know where what we have between us will lead; all I know is that I feel closer to you than anyone else in the world. And I want to make *us* work. I don't have to work in Antarctica. I thought I could get a job improving communication systems for remote First Nations communities and small outback towns. There's bound to be some kind of government program already in place – otherwise, I'll seek private funding. I'm certain my father would be able to put me in touch with the right people to organise. The other part of the year – maybe we could travel. We could make Sturt Crossing our base. Imagine the vlogs you could post. You could bring the hardships these communities face every day to the eyes of the people of the world."

Pressing his cheek to hers, he repeated the words he longed with all his heart would come true. "Come with me and we'll travel under the Outback sky together."

CHAPTER

SIXTEEN

P ulse thumping like the drumming of an emu racing over hard-packed earth Maggie tugged her hands free and, shifting closer, placed them on his chest. His skin was warm and smooth through the thin fabric of his shirt, and she longed to slide her fingers over his bare skin. She felt giddy with a heady swirl of excitement and hope. All kinds of possibilities teased her mind but the one that took centre place was the lure of a life spent by the side of a man she found both fascinating and honourable.

Finally, she became aware Jace had rushed into speech again.

"If you decide that you can't leave, I will understand. But you're not getting away from me so easily. I'll fly in and out to jobs and still make this place my home base. If you'll have me, of course," he added in a gruff voice.

She laid a finger on his lips cutting off the flow of words. "I've already told my parents that they'll have to find someone else to manage their store."

"Really? How did they react? What...?"

Her hands slipped around his neck, loving the feel of his hard body against hers and chuckled. "Complete and utter surprise. But as soon as they learned I was serious, they couldn't have been more supportive."

"So you've told them...what exactly?"

"That I intend to hunt you down in Antarctica and make you mine."

"Now that is something I'd like to see. But no need darling, I'm already yours. I think I was the first time we met." Jace grinned, then flung his head back and let loose a joyous laugh before claiming her mouth with a kiss that burned straight through to her heart.

Passion flared, burning bright and strong. Through her palms she felt his heartbeat quicken, heard the rapid sound of his breathing, felt his heat searing her body. Her knees went weak as her belly turned to liquid. She clung to him, the kiss deepening becoming something more than love and desire – something like a never-ending promise. She had found her dream man – or maybe he had found her.

His hands roamed her body with an eagerness that delighted and inflamed her already heightened senses as his mouth moved along her cheek then down her neck. Gliding his tongue over her skin, he teased the sensitive lobe of her ear. She trembled, sliding her hands beneath his shirt to explore his firm pectoral muscles. Tonight, there would be no going back. Finally! The thought was enough for a girl to want to scream *'hallelujah'*!

Stepping backwards, she tugged him to follow and they stumbled their way towards the door. Maggie groped for the handle behind her and was just about to wrench it open when someone called out. There came the crunch of footsteps on pebbles and the squeak of a wheel. Sherman gave an excited wuff and scurried across the boards and down the steps.

Jace lifted his head, breathing hard, his eyes glazed and molten with a heady desire that made her quiver inside. "Don't tell me – it's someone with another casserole."

She squeezed her own eyes shut for a second willing her racing pulse to slow then stared ruefully into his lightly flushed face. "I think that's my parents coming."

"I'm going to have to say something to them about their timing." Jace slid his hands off her reluctantly and took a step away, shoving them into his pants pocket. "I hope they won't think I'm rude but I'm in no condition to face them after that kiss."

Maggie giggled. "Stand behind me. I'll protect you."

"Cheeky." He leaned in and pressed his lips ever so tenderly to the spot beside her mouth. "You're so beautiful and I'm the luckiest man alive."

"I know." She winked then shifted so she stood in front of him waiting for her parents to reach the bottom of the veranda stairs. "Mum. Dad. I thought you'd gone to bed."

"After that conversation? Hell no. We've got things to discuss." Grant craned his neck to try to get a good look at Jace, a sly grin stealing over his face. "No guesses as to what you two have been up to. You got anything to say to us, young man?"

Jace cleared his throat. "Well...I want to marry your daughter if she'll have me."

"Marriage?" Maggie swung to face him.

"What can I say?" He shrugged. "I'm old-fashioned and I've realised I want to share your dream, Maggie mine. The forever-kind of life with a football team of kids."

"Did you hear that, Lucy? We're going to be grand-parents!" hollered her father.

"I can't wait to tell the CWA girls!" gushed her mother as she scooped Sherman into her arms to give him an affectionate cuddle.

The door opened behind her and out bustled Mr. McKenzie with a bottle in his hand so fast that Maggie suspected he'd been listening in from the hallway. "I knew it! Got the champagne from Snake yesterday." He popped the cork and held the bottle high in his hand. "Let's drink to the happy couple."

Jace whispered in her ear, "Looks like our alone time is going to be postponed – again."

"It better happen soon, or I'm going to combust!"

"Same," he growled, taking possession of her lips in a hungry kiss.

"We need glasses," declared Brian McKenzie. "Now, leave the girl alone Jace and help your father-in-law to be up those stairs." After placing the champagne on the table, he disappeared back into the house.

"Yes sir." Grinning Jace moved to obey while Lucy surged forward to embrace her daughter.

"I'm so happy for you Margaret."

"Thanks, Mum."

A few seconds later, they were all gathered around holding glasses brimming with bubbly.

"A toast to my lovely daughter and my future son-in-law." Grant raised his glass and shot Lucy a quick glance. She nodded then he spoke again. "No need to worry about us, pet. We've got plenty of friends to help us out and we'll get either Glen or maybe Mosa Botha to mind the store when we're off attending rehab. I'm sure Mrs. Botha could do with the extra money. Your mother and I have had a talk and we're offering you the RV to use if you wish for the next twelve months." In the hand he held out, lay a set of car keys.

"You mean it?" Not giving them time to change their minds, Maggie snatched the keys and held them close. "This will be perfect for us. Thanks Mum, Dad." Leaning over she hugged her parents while Jace offered his own thanks, pumping her father's hand then giving her mother a kiss on the cheek.

"What are your plans? How soon will you be off?" asked Mr. McKenzie from where he sat in one of the cane chairs fiddling with the stem of his wine glass.

Maggie exchanged a questioning glance at Jace before saying, "We haven't decided, but probably within the next couple of days. I'm not sure how long we'll be away for but I can't imagine never coming home to Sturt's Crossing. First though, we need to go to Melbourne where Jace's family lives."

He caught her hand in his and linked their fingers together. Smiling, he said, "Unfinished business to take care of. I have an apartment there which has a small community garden for kids and pets so accommodation is all sorted. Although we'll have to get strata approval for Sherman, I'm certain that won't be a problem. I can't wait to show Maggie the sights and take her out to dinner in some posh restaurant."

"And meet your parents." She grinned back at him.

An annoyed frown settled over her mother's face. "But what about the wedding? When's that to be? There is no way you are getting married without your family present!"

"Mum!" Heat scalded Maggie's cheeks. "We haven't had time to talk about anything like that yet."

"Don't worry, Mrs. Hayes." Jace smiled at Maggie. "Sturt's Crossing sounds perfect to me."

Maggie could have hugged herself with joy. Another dream coming true. A little of her happiness dimmed as she remembered the threat to her beloved hometown and sipped her champagne. "But before we leave town we still need to discover who is working for the mining company."

Her father shook his head and snorted. "No need. That will be Charlie and Larry's doing for sure. They've been sending soil and rock samples off to various mining companies for years. Always hoping they'll hit the jackpot and be rewarded with a pile of money. Idiots, the pair of them."

Maggie stared. "Are you certain, Dad?"

"Yup. No need to stress about it, pet. Ask Mrs. Stillman at the post office. She'll be able to tell you how many times she's had to mail packages for those two clowns."

"Well, I'd never believe it if you hadn't told me, Dad.

They've been some of the most vocal people urging us to sign petitions! The whole town has been worried for weeks!"

"Like I said, idiots." Grant upended his glass and took a massive gulp. "Good bubbly this. Thanks, Brian."

"My pleasure. Nothing like happy endings." The elderly gent gave a wistful smile as if his thoughts were far away.

Jace placed his glass on the table then pulled Maggie into his arms. Exultation, joy and something like hope glowed in his dark eyes. "Not endings – this is only the beginning."

She wrapped her arms around his neck and snuggled close. "One that I can't wait to begin. I love you, Jace."

"Ditto, Maggie mine. Let's begin here." Then ignoring the smiling on-lookers, he kissed her.

THANK **you** or purchasing ***Under an Outback Sky***. I hope you enjoyed reading Jace and Maggie's story.

The other books written by me in this world are: ***Cowboy Under the Mistletoe, Dance in the Outback*** and ***The Cowboy's Gift.***

IF YOU ENJOYED ***Under an Outback Sky*** **you may also enjoy** *Take Me Home* **from the Bindarra Creek Romance series.**

Excerpt from *Take Me Home* © *Suzanne Gilchrist 2019*

CHAPTER 1

The icy winter night closed in around the paddy wagon, the instant Senior Constable Abigail Taylor killed the engine. Shivering as the heater died and the gusty wind rocked the car on its axles, she pulled her navy-blue beanie over her blonde hair then glanced across at Senior Sergeant Riley Morgan.

"Looks like we have company." Abby nodded to where three figures could be seen, shoulders hunched in their winter coats, hands deep in their pockets, as they stamped their feet on the front porch of Bindarra Creek Police Station.

The security lighting did little to discern their features, hidden beneath hoods pulled low over their faces. An adult and a couple of kids, thought Abby, as she took a sharp visual inventory. The kids kept their backs to the adult, standing a good three metres away as if to emphasise they didn't belong as a unit. Possibly an irate home-owner who had caught the kids in the act of desecrating his fence with graffiti - all in the name of art - or boredom.

More paperwork. More soothing of ruffled feathers. More kids to place on 'clean-up' duty. She bit back her sigh, her hopes of catching the bistro at the Riverside Pub before it closed, disappearing like Halley's Comet over the horizon.

Riley rubbed a hand over his stubbly jaw and mumbled past a wide yawn, "I'll see to it."

Smiling, Abby released her seat belt and slipped the

keys from the ignition. "Nope. Leave it to me, boss. You've got a full night ahead of you with that baby of yours."

"Teething!" He groaned. "Never thought baby teeth could cause so much pain."

Ignoring the savage momentary twist of jealousy that gripped her, Abby managed a grin. "For you or the kid?"

"All of us." Meeting her gaze, Riley grimaced. "I'm on night duty tonight while Sam gets some sleep."

"All the more reason for me to deal with whoever is on our front doorstep."

"Thanks. I'll give you a hand, writing up tonight's incident in the morning."

"Sounds like a plan." Eager to avoid any more talk about children, Abby grabbed her thick police-issue jacket from the back of the seat while Riley climbed out the other side of the wagon.

With a brief wave, she pushed open the car door then leaned heavily against it as the wind slammed it back toward her body. "Ouch. I'll be so glad to get out of this weather."

"You okay?" Riley placed his hand on the bonnet.

"Yeah, all good. Thanks. See you bright and early." She pushed her arms into the sleeves of her jacket while Riley sprinted towards the highway patrol car and climbed inside.

A few moments later, his car's taillights disappeared down the road – heading for home. Heading for a hot dinner that was no doubt waiting for him. But definitely heading home to his family.

Family. Something Abby no longer had in her life.

Burying her brief flash of sadness, she turned to the small group waiting for her. With her hands resting lightly on her gel duty belt, she strode the short distance through a buffeting wind so cold it made her eyes water and her nose numb. She lifted her gaze briefly to the dark sky where clouds scudded across the scattering of stars. Too high to portend any rain, unfortunately. The region could do with a good downfall. But an early morning frost could well be on the cards. In other words, a very chilly night.

Flexing her stiff fingers, she stopped on the top step, her heart doing a crazy skip as she recognised the adult. "Elizabeth! What are you doing here?"

~

ACKNOWLEDGMENTS

My special thanks go to Sandie James for her time in critiquing my manuscript and giving me some valuable suggestions. I also wish to thank Ann B Harrison for encouraging me to finish Maggie and Jace's story during a difficult time in my life. Thank you also to Cindy Pearson for her wonderful proofreading skills.

In order to achieve authenticity when mentioning the *Legend of the Sturt Desert Pea*, several websites were researched. Any inaccuracies are entirely the fault of the author and are unintentional. Accordingly, I thank and acknowledge the following:

https://www.madonnamagazine.com.au/aboriginal-legend-sturt-desert-pea-elizabeth-pike/

https://ausemade.com.au/art-culture/aboriginal-art-culture/aboriginal-dreaming/flowers-of-blood/

https://www.gadimirrabooka.com/aboriginal-stories/23-33/sturt-desert-pea

https://nativesymbols.info/sturts-desert-pea/

About the Author

S. E. Gilchrist can't remember a time when she didn't have a book in her hand. Now she dreams up stories where her favourite words are ... 'what if' and 'where'? Writing as both S. E. Gilchrist and Suzanne Gilchrist, she loves combining romance with adventure and suspense across many different genres including space opera, apocalyptic, and contemporary small towns.
S. E. takes a keen interest in the environment, anything to do with space, and loves walking her two dogs and spending time with her family and friends. She co-runs the Hunter Romance Writers group and is the organiser behind the multi-author writing ventures: the best-selling Bindarra Creek Romance series, the Deadly Forces series, and the Mindalby Outback Romance series.

For more information, visit her website:
https:www.segilchrist.com